M000080924

Bowman's Line

Bowman's
Line

Bowman's Line

BRIAN ANDREW LAIRD

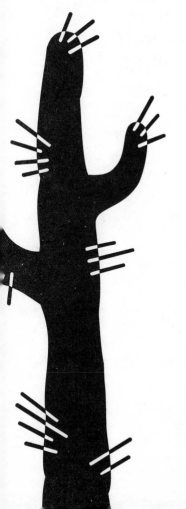

St. Martin's Press
New York

BOWMAN'S LINE. Copyright © 1995 by Brian Andrew Laird. All rights reserved. Printed in the United States of America. No part of this book may be used or reproduced in any manner whatsoever without written permission except in the case of brief quotations embodied in critical articles or reviews. For information, address St. Martin's Press, 175 Fifth Avenue, New York, N.Y. 10010.

Library of Congress Cataloging-in-Publication Data

Laird, Brian Andrew.
    Bowman's line / Brian Andrew Laird.
       p.   cm.
    "A Thomas Dunne Book."
    ISBN 0-312-13033-3
    I. Title.
PS3562.A354B68   1995
813'.54—dc20   95-2822

                          CIP

First edition: August 1995

10 9 8 7 6 5 4 3 2 1

For lovely Wendi Irene Kulin

. . . and

for Larry Powell,
one of the great ones

Thanks to my editor, Ruth Cavin, and to St. Martin's Press. To Jeanne Williams, for advice, encouragement and assistance. To Betty Roberton Fielden and L.C.P. for continuous support.

To Geoff Gould and Scott Durgan, whom I leaned on heavily in the bad times, and to Martina too.

To Lee Sewell, who was there all along. To Joseph Romanov, my oldest friend. To the McHenrys, Chuck, Cindy, and all.

To Wendy Laird, for support and assistance. To the Huggins gang—Cynthia, Jesse, J. Allan, and Justine. To David and Kathy and Kristine and Eric, Lairds all. To Linda Laird and Larry Haney. To my grandparents. And to W.D. Laird for getting me started in the right direction.

To Stephanie Heiman, for passing through at just the right time. To Robert Hershoff and Cecil Wellborn, great bookmen both. To Bob Pugh, Arizona's bookscout. And to Nancy Gullet, lovingly.

To Chip Sonenblick, for the childhood memories—too little, too late.

To Bunny Fontana, historian extraordinaire. To Julian Hayden, for example.

And to Chuck Bowden, for not coming after me with a shotgun.

Bowman's
Line

Prologue

He looked down at his trembling hands. They were scratched and dirty. Blood streaked through the uneven layer of brown soil, webbing his shaking fingers in crooked lines of black.

There was only one big cut, and that was good. He wasn't going to bleed to death, anyway. But he could see the thick, flat pad of soft flesh speckled with brown dirt crumbs, sliced open and quivering with each pounding heartbeat. Then the blood quickly filled the gap, like liquid sucked into an empty syringe, and spilled out over his palm.

He pinched the wound closed, squeezing out the blood, pressing the hand tightly to his waist, where his belt should have been. He held the hand firmly there. His breath came in great heaves, and he chanted quietly.

"Do it . . . do it . . . do it . . ." he urged himself.

He pulled the hand away from his naked waist. Again the soft pink flesh trembled with his heartbeat, then pooled quickly with blood.

His gaze shot right and left, looking for something with which to bandage the wound. Nothing. And there would be nothing ahead. Only trees and rock, the forest stretching for two or three more miles above.

There would be just one small break in the woods, for the radio towers—an oasis in the evergreen emptiness of this stretch of the Coronado National Forest, high above the sprawling desert city.

If he had clothes—a shirt, pants, anything—he could tear off a strip of fabric and wrap it tightly around the wound. He glanced down at his naked body, scratched and bleeding, and pale in the moonlight where skin showed through the dirt he had rubbed all over himself.

He knew that the only way to stop the bleeding was to squeeze the wound closed with his other hand. That meant moving slowly, or running awkwardly, hands clasped in front of him, increasing the risk of tripping again, unable to break the fall this time, unable to stop a stick or sharp rock from slicing into a more vital place.

If he were cut like this at one of the soft spots inside his arms and legs, or at his neck, near a major artery, he would be in much worse shape. He would, in fact, be dead very quickly.

The fear welled up in his throat again, and he felt like whimpering. He shook his head sharply from side to side, willing the terror away.

Then once more he heard the noise behind him. And he ran.

He ignored the hand and the blood and the pain, and he scrambled through the hard, scratching branches of the pines. His feet landed on solid ground, then pressed into thick pine needles.

Sometimes he kicked rocks or stepped down on sharp, dead tree branches, breaking already broken toes, and cutting already cut feet.

The desert upon which they were entrained was desert absolute and it was devoid of feature altogether and there was nothing to mark their progress upon it.

Cormac McCarthy
Blood Meridian

*There is something more in the desert,
something that has no name.*

Edward Abbey
Beyond the Wall

We are left to the silence. It is absolute.

Charles Bowden
Red Line

One

It's simple, Bowman wrote. *Out there in the desert
you face something that has been inside you all
along. Some call it fear. It has other names, tainted
by our superstitions—religion and culture. Some
know it for evil. In any case, it is a monster. And
either you crush it, or it devours you.*

Bowman stumbled out of the brush, falling to one knee on
the hard shoulder of the highway.

Highway. If you wanted to call it that. The asphalt, broken and patched, then broken and left that way, had been
laid fifty years ago with the limited funds of a third-world
nation. It was just a thin strip of crumbling tar and gravel a
hundred miles long, running from the hot, angry town of
Cancione, Mexico, to the Arizona border.

Bowman pushed himself up from the scorching surface.
His face was pale and thin. Sweat had broken out and dried,
then broken out again many times, and his headband and
clothes were covered with receding white lines of body
salt—like tide markers to the walk that had almost killed
him.

He was clammy and shaking. He felt dehydrated, close
to heat stroke, and his skin had begun to take on the lifeless
feel of rubber. He was aware that he had been hallucinating
for some time now. He gazed up the thin strip of asphalt.

This was the Devil's Highway.

It roughly paralleled an ancient path that had been used for hundreds, maybe thousands, of years. Father Kino had walked here, the first white man to do it, looking for an overland route to California, proselytizing the Indians on the way, like a great player in the big con patiently setting up the mark.

The path started in the low flatlands just above the gulf and stretched north and west to the edge of the big river. Not long after Kino's day, those lands would be irrigated, eventually becoming northern Mexico's breadbasket. But then it was just hard, barren ground, baking under the desert sun.

From the flatlands the path headed north and west into the desert wilderness. There was water at Cancione and Las Hambres.

Then nothing.

After Las Hambres, there was just the hard, hot desert.

The only water for a hundred miles might be found at the *tinajas*—small grooves atop the Pinacate Mountains, carved into the stone by countless desert storms. Getting to the *tinajas* took a hard, dangerous climb up craggy volcanic rock.

If a man were very thirsty and out of water, he might risk the climb. Sometimes water could be found there, pooled after a short, furious Sonoran rainstorm. Sometimes.

But if the *tinajas* were dry, he would stand atop the Pinacates and look down on a huge stretch of black, hostile rock, alkaline ground, and cactus. And he would begin to panic.

In the summer, temperatures reached a hundred and

thirty degrees by midday, and the ground radiated long after dark, cooling to eighty-five or ninety degrees just before dawn. Without water, a man could last for a day, maybe two.

The bones of countless mules and packhorses littered the path, victims of the desert's rage. The bones of men returned to the earth alongside them. The desert did not discriminate.

In the summer, the road belonged to the devil.

It was summer now, and Bowman looked down at his palms, scraped through to flesh. Not too bad really, not much blood. How many times had he been scraped and scratched, cut by the desert's sharp skin? He couldn't count the number.

The knee was worse. Two nights ago he had cut it badly while running on a jagged bank of volcanic rock in the dark. Going full tilt, he had fallen, landing mostly on the knee. The gash had swollen quickly, draining blood and fluid all night and most of the next day.

Now he'd broken it open again, and thin blood flowed out, covering his shin.

Bowman slipped his backpack off, let it fall in the dirt behind him. Somewhere inside the overstuffed black canvas pack was a first-aid kit with sterile pads, antibiotic ointment, and tape. But he was just too tired to look for it now, nearly ravaged by the heat. Instead, he pulled off his T-shirt. It was soiled with three day's sweat and dirt, and blood. Blood not his own.

He wrapped the filthy cotton shirt twice around the wound, knotting it in front.

The photographer would have laughed. The photographer would have ranked Bowman with a litany on infection, gangrene, and amputation. He would have told Bowman the small effort was probably worth it to avoid a prosthesis later.

That didn't matter now. The photographer was dead.

Two

It had been dark, and a scramble up to the *tinajas* dangerous. But they had been scrambling for their lives.

They were dehydrated, demoralized, devoured by the heat.

A couple of hours before, Bowman had crawled out from under the branches of the low bush where he'd been sleeping—a fitful, half-conscious sleep that provided no rest, no relief, allowed only for a half-aware kind of endurance.

They had not been prepared for it. In all the trips through Sonora that they had made on foot or in vehicles, they had not encountered heat like this. This was a heat beyond heat. Heat that penetrated deep inside the skin until it seemed to overtake and possess, and Bowman had felt no longer himself, but lost and only a part of the heat, the heat everywhere and the man himself just a shimmering wave of heat shifting above the lava, ash, and sand.

The photographer had lain on his back, mostly shaded by the brush. His face was pale and dry, his mouth open in a wretched, silent scream—a mime imitating death. Bowman detected no movement until he walked near; then he saw the chest moving slowly up and down, the nostrils flaring with each breath.

He'd nudged the photographer with his foot.

"Huhn, what the hell?" The photographer blinked groggily.

"Time to get up, Romeo," Bowman said in a raspy voice.

"Wish you'd let me go just a few more minutes. I was having a hell of a dream."

And that, thought Bowman, sums up John Vyking— purebred desert rat, world-class photographer, fearless and talented—the kind of man who would crack jokes on the road to his own funeral.

"If we don't make it to the *tinajas* and find some water, you'll get to sleep the sleep of the just—the just plain dead." Bowman said.

The photographer nodded. They both understood. The wisecracks were a sign that both believed the situation had become perilous.

Usually, communication between them was strictly functional: Does this route go over that rise, or do we stick to the valley? How much food is left? How far to the trail's head? It was one of the reasons they worked so well together. Neither liked small talk. Each left the other alone, to do his job.

The barbed comments, they knew, were cover for something quite different inside. They were scared.

Bowman had one canteen left, the photographer two. Early that morning, with the sun already beating him nearly senseless, Bowman had tripped and fallen flat on a jagged mesquite root. One canteen had swung between him and the sharp stick, preventing the root from puncturing the soft flesh of his belly.

As he rose, the canteen began to leak—half of his most

precious resource disappearing into the hungry desert sand. He'd called for Vyking and then held the canteen high above his head, drinking half of its contents before passing it to his partner.

Watching the photographer drink, Bowman had joked that it might have been better if he'd punctured himself with the stick. "I don't have any blood left anyway."

They'd chuckled grimly at that, but even then, the two men had known that things were getting perilous. The heat was worse than they had thought it would be. At least a hundred and twenty-five degrees on the sandy ground in the wash, maybe hotter.

Forty miles to the south, there was a highway. Could they make it that far? They talked it over and agreed they probably couldn't. Instead, they had kept on north, but by mid-afternoon, with less than a gallon of water left, it had become clear that they were in trouble.

They had dropped their backpacks, tucked them under a paloverde by the arroyo, the deadweight of food, clothing, and camera equipment useless to them now.

The *tinajas* lay a few miles ahead. They would sleep through the hottest part of the afternoon, then go there. At the *tinajas* they would fill all three canteens, rest until night cooled the oven around them, then head south, a forty-mile forced march to the potholed Mexican highway.

They had crawled into the sparse shade and fallen to fitful sleep.

Now, with the sun setting, they rose and split what was left of the water, emptying the canteen.

"Got to get moving," Vyking said.

"No time like right now."

"And if we get out of here, there won't be again. Walk the Camino del Diablo in summer, you said, a great adventure, a great story." The photographer scowled. "Never again."

They both laughed a little.

"I like your company—your charm, your wit."

"Which way?"

"North," Bowman said, pointing.

"Easy enough."

"Better get there before nightfall. It'll be harder to find in the dark."

"Just a second." Vyking pulled a camera and a flash unit from his pack, slung them over one shoulder. It was one of his habits. It was, in fact, his prime directive, his First Commandment: Thou Shalt Carry Camera Equipment. He pulled the two canteens over his shoulder as well.

"Time for some *Tinajas Tecate*," he said, and they walked north.

The two men scrambled up the last few feet of volcanic rock in the moonless night.

This, they figured, was their last chance. All the lower pools had been empty, as dry as any sand. They'd paused to rest for the final climb, leaning back against the hard, craggy slope. Panting dryly, Bowman looked out over the desert, an emptiness of darkening scrub.

Then, silently, they picked their way to the top.

Nothing. The last of the *tinajas* was as dry as the others—a hot stone pit stained with pale lines of sediment.

For a moment, Bowman felt himself clutched in the hard claws of panic. His heart began to pound.

He closed his eyes, looked inside, took stock of himself. *Stay in control,* he told himself. *Just keep it together. You're not dead yet.*

He squeezed the panic away, and felt his pounding heart begin to slow.

"Nate." The photographer was a few feet above him, looking down at the dark desert basin on the far side of the hill. "Nate, I'll be damned if there's not someone down there."

Bowman turned slowly and climbed up the rock. He stared out over the black and empty landscape. Now he saw it too. At the bottom of the slope, half-hidden in an escarpment, beams of light played on the hillside.

Bowman started over the edge, set to scramble down after help. The photographer grabbed his shoulder, pulled him back.

Bowman turned on Vyking, ready to protest, but then he saw the look, the pursed lips, the finger held up for quiet, and he understood. There were very few people who wandered this area of the borderlands, especially at night, and most of them wouldn't welcome uninvited guests.

They followed the ridge down a rough slope and around an outcropping of mottled black rock. They had dropped the canteens back at the *tinajas,* and the photographer carried the camera and flash slung behind him, around his neck and one shoulder.

Past the outcropping, the slope played off in two directions; a sharp drop to the western floor of the desert, and to the east, a gentle slope twisting back to a shallow canyon that disappeared beneath the far side of the mountain.

Vyking led as they descended the slope, picking their way carefully, slowly, over the rocky ground. They approached the lip of the canyon, and the photographer pointed across the ridge. They climbed the rise and moved out toward the rim of the shallow canyon.

From their perch, Bowman could see the thin, clear strip of sand running crossways through the canyon below them, a jeep trail that twisted off into the blackness to the southeast.

Near the edge, he looked down into the shallow canyon. Just below them—how far? Two hundred, two hundred and fifty feet? Bowman couldn't judge for certain in the darkness, but here the rocks opened up and the canyon widened.

He and the photographer were in line with the spot where they had stood atop of the *tinajas,* and when they crept up to the rim, crouching low, they had a clear view of the flashlight beams swinging across the canyon floor.

Men moved about down there at a clipped, serious pace. The flashlights played mostly on one vehicle. Bowman could make it out clearly. A longbed truck with wide, dual rear wheels. The truck apparently had come up the trail from the southeast, and it was parked where the road ended at a cleft in the earth.

To the north, the canyon opened up and the ground smoothed out. A long, bulky vehicle sat on the flat land beyond the opening, and the men hauled load after load to the truck from the . . . what? Bowman couldn't quite make it out. He shielded his eyes, crossing his hands beneath them, palms down, like a man balancing an invisible pair of binoculars on his fingertips, and blocked out the flashlight beams. Now he could see it. A light aircraft. Twin engine. Propeller.

If there had been any doubt that he and the photographer were observing a smuggling operation, Bowman felt sure it was eliminated.

Two people stood by the plane. One had dark hair cut short. The other was taller and bald. They did not help the mules unload the cargo.

Just beyond the flashlight beams, one of the mules stumbled and fell. A light swung his way, revealing the dropped load. The bag had split open, and some of its contents poured out on the dirt.

Under the flashlight beam the white substance shone in sharp contrast to the blackness all around. Someone shouted orders in Spanish.

"He's telling them to pick it up," the photographer whispered.

The mules moved quickly, scooping up little white chunks by the handful and pouring them into the bag. A light, hot breeze shifted through the brush, lifting the dry scent to Bowman's nose. He felt a tingling in the membranes. The accompanying urge to sneeze seized him.

The photographer looked at Bowman and saw his scrunched-up face pulling back for the burst of lung air. Vyking reached out and clipped Bowman's nose between finger and thumb and squeezed hard. Hard enough to hurt. When he pulled his hand away, Bowman relaxed.

He rubbed his nose gently and gave the photographer a reproachful look, but Vyking had already turned his attention back to the canyon floor. He eased his camera around his shoulder and tucked it firmly up to his right eye.

Bowman winced as the photographer's finger squeezed

down on the shutter release, expecting the telltale snapping noise and the whir of an electric motor. Instead, the shutter flipped with the softest of clicks, like a hitched breath, and the photographer pulled the camera from his cheek to carefully wind the frame forward by hand.

As they crouched there, Vyking snapped off a dozen more shots in the hushed night, then rewound and removed the film cartridge, replacing it with another. Bowman's gaze returned to the scene below, and he wondered how the photographer could get a decent exposure from the wavering beams of the flashlights.

Vyking touched Bowman's shoulder to get his attention and indicated with a nod to move back from the edge. For a second time that night, the photographer pressed a finger to his pursed lips. This time Bowman nodded, understanding. The two men retreated from the canyon edge.

They stepped carefully into the darkness, following the ridge back in the direction from which they had come. A few hundred feet up the embankment, the photographer pushed Bowman behind a large outcropping of volcanic rock.

"Fucking mules," Vyking whispered.

"Probably don't want any company," Bowman rasped.

"They'd eat us for an early breakfast. A light breakfast at that," he added with a weary grin.

"How can you get photos in that light?"

"Very sensitive film, sixty-four hundred, and slow shutter speed. It's all in holding the thing steady enough. But I got it. Good pictures of the mules and the truck, even got the markings on the plane."

"And the noise?"

"What noise?"

"The silence, then. I kept expecting the clack of a shutter closing."

"It has a setting that muffles the noise, holds the mirror up. That's what makes all the noise, the mirror flapping up."

"What now?" Bowman asked.

"Hell, I don't know."

The dilemma was clear. No water at the *tinajas*. None left in their canteens. Both believed it would not be possible to cross the desert to the highway from here. Not in their exhausted, dehydrated condition.

But there was simply no way to get help from the people below. Bowman and Vyking would be under suspicion just by their presence here.

Bowman imagined trying to explain what they were doing out here—walking an ancient desert trail, retracing the *jornadas* of so many before them—*jornadas de los muertos*.

To Bowman, it suddenly seemed preposterous. Who would do such a thing? How would it sound to a drug smuggler, to someone living in a state of constant paranoia, on the fringe of society? It would sound like a lie, and not even a very good one. He could imagine the response. *Sure. Sure, señor. Of course you are walking El Camino del Diablo. We all are, que no? But this story you are working on, perhaps it is really about something else. Perhaps it is about the, what, the export business en la frontera? Or perhaps there is no story. Perhaps you are not a journalist, but this is only, how do you say . . . your cover? It is common for many agents of your Drug Enforcement Agency to say they are journalists. But they are not. I think you are not.*

It would be a nightmare, and it would end with their

deaths, their bodies left in the desert, maybe never to be found.

"What do you say we wait until they go?" Vyking finally suggested. "See if they leave anything behind."

"I can't think of anything better. Unless you'd consider marching down there and confiscating their airplane."

"We wait," the photographer said.

And that's when he made his mistake.

It was the photographer's only miscue, the first Bowman had seen him make. In all their travels together it had always been the photographer who was competent and careful, and Bowman who crashed headlong into the fray.

"I'm going to shoot another roll," Vyking had whispered as he reloaded the camera. He fumbled a little, trying to get the film to catch in the spindle. As he bent over, the flash unit swung clunkily in front of him, further mucking up the situation. He grunted and shoved the flash back out of the way.

Finally, camera loaded, they both moved carefully back down the ridge to their observation point. Bowman hung back, and as the photographer crawled out to the ridge, Bowman whispered roughly to him in the darkness.

"Watch the rocks," he said.

"What?" The photographer asked, and as he turned back toward Bowman, the flash unit swung around again and struck the camera in his hands.

The bright, white flash of light closely approximated a silent nuclear explosion. At least it did for Bowman and the photographer, their eyes fully adjusted to the dark, and now instantly, if temporarily, blinded. It left them both with fluctuating green after-images bathing their vision.

For the men in the distance, it was both signal flare and target beacon.

There were shouts from below in both Spanish and English.

Bowman dropped to the ground, rubbing his eyes and backing away from the edge.

The photographer stayed on his feet, scrambling backward over the scrub.

The snap of distant gunfire erupted, and a flashlight beam swung across the hillside, weakened by distance and scarcely illuminating anything.

Then more shouts, a single, high-pitched voice rising in Spanish above the others, and the gunfire ceased.

Bowman's eyes adjusted quickly, and he and Vyking scrambled up the slope, heading for the safety of the large outcropping of rock.

He no longer felt the effects of dehydration and fatigue. Adrenaline coursed through his body as he made the panicked dash. This was what it was like, he realized, to fear as a child does. To fear the unknown. To fear death.

He ducked his head and charged up the slope, lungs pumping harsh blasts of hot air.

The photographer was a few steps behind, moving a little slower, his short legs working against him, covering less ground.

The rock was just ahead. Bowman could see its jagged outline silhouetted against the incredibly bright stars of the Sonoran sky.

There was a flash in his peripheral vision. He glanced back over his shoulder and saw the beam of a hand-operated spotlight sweeping the hillside.

Then he was at the outcropping. He took one last great stride and burst around the corner. Behind him, the beam froze, locked on the spot where he had topped the rise. Bowman tumbled to the ground, looking back.

For a blazing, white-hot second, the scene stood still. The brilliant light. The crags of the rock, lit as clear as day where the light hit them, every shadow in sharp contrast. The soft whiteness beyond. And the photographer, in perfect silhouette, lunging forward.

Then Vyking was jerking in a mindless dance, to the sound of gunfire in the distance.

He fell forward and slid limply down the hillside.

Bowman moved to him, knelt at his side. The photographer's breath was a sickening wet rattle.

Bowman's breath came in great panicked gulps. Hands trembling, he gently turned Vyking over.

The photographer gagged and coughed, and blood spewed out of his mouth like rusty water from a garden hose.

"Damn!" Bowman panted. "Goddamnit, John, goddamnit!"

The photographer clucked his jaw up and down, trying to form words.

"Oh shit, John. Shit, it's bad," Bowman said.

The photographer worked his mouth again and finally rasped out a word with great effort.

"Film." Then he closed his eyes, breathing out heavily, finally.

The searchlight swept back and forth across the ridge above them, and Bowman heard men scrambling up the other side, shouting to each other in Spanish.

Bowman searched Vyking's shirt pockets and located the stubby plastic cylinder. Vyking's chest was motionless, the body lifeless beneath Bowman's hands.

Again the light swept over the jagged crest of the slope. The shouts were closer. And another noise. A growing whine in the background.

Bowman turned, his mind a blur, terrified and defenseless, looking madly down the western slope. It was the dead of night, and he could see almost nothing down there. He stood, and for the first time he noticed his knee, split open and bleeding where he had fallen.

The noise grew louder, a low-pitched, steady scream. Bowman hunched down, ducking the assault of the piercing sound.

Then the airplane rose above the ridge, and it banked hard, heading north and east, its lights flashing.

Bowman heard the mules working their way up the hillside, and saw the flashlights growing brighter. He tucked the film into the pocket of his jeans and crashed down the steep slope into the night, like a man starved for darkness.

Three

The flatbed stopped where the road forked. Downtown Sonoyta. All dirt and crumbling sidewalks, and buildings painted a fading aquamarine.

Bowman climbed slowly from the truckbed, easing onto his good leg first. It had been a couple of hours since the truck stopped for him. A couple of hours bouncing down the rough road, resting on top of the springless chunk of rusted steel, and his knee was stiff and swollen.

The ride had been quiet. A few broken questions from the *campesinos* he rode with, then nothing. The hardworking, tough-skinned men spoke little English. Bowman spoke less Spanish.

It was one of the things he sometimes wondered at, that he could travel as much as he did in Mexico—three or four months a year hiking across and along the border—and still not know the language. It was incredible. But true. And after a few frustrating attempts, he had given up trying to learn.

The men had talked quietly, their deep brown skin shining under the sun, black hair splashing in the wind. Their

25

clothes, cleaner than Bowman's, were stained and tattered, patched and repatched like the road they traveled on.

Bowman didn't feel much like talking anyway. He needed time to rest, and to think. After escaping the *tinajas,* he had stumbled around until he found his backpack. He'd tugged the thing onto his shoulders, figuring that if he had any chance of making it out of the desert alive, he would need the first-aid supplies and food packets stored there. Then he'd wandered across the Sonoran wilderness in the dark, and sometime just before dawn, when he could go no farther, he'd crawled under a bush and fallen into a fitful sleep.

He'd slept through the morning and well into the afternoon, and when he woke, it was not the light, but the sudden shift in temperature and the darkening sky that pulled him to consciousness. Then the wind came up, the sky tore open, and rain poured down. And even as he'd scrambled to get a plastic container from his pack and let it fill with rainfall, Bowman had known he would make it to the highway.

One of the *campesinos* leaned over the truck's wooden rail to lower Bowman's backpack.

"La frontera," the man said, pointing up the road.

"Gracias."

The man dropped back into the bed of the truck, and as the transmission clanked and caught gear, the conversation suddenly grew lively.

Bowman turned toward the border with a thin smile. Mexico was an enigma. Where else would a bunch of working stiffs give a ride to a man they thought could get them arrested?

To the *campesinos,* Bowman clearly looked like a smuggler, or anyway, a *loco*—a fool, a madman. Certainly he was trouble. But he was also, as evident by his pale skin and backpack, a visitor, and he'd needed a ride. So they had picked him up, taken a chance, given him a hand. Like their neighbors, the O'Odham—the People of the Earth, Native Americans who shared northern Sonora and baja Arizona with them—the *campesinos* of Mexico had the understated dignity of a simple life.

He stopped, shifted his pack, and with one hand wiped the sweat from his forehead and nose. The border was just ahead, a few hundred yards farther.

This was the tough part. You could walk a hundred miles straight toward this place and none of it would be as touch-and-go as the last few feet. Not if you looked like Bowman.

Tall and rangy, growing a little padding at the middle, mostly from tequila and beer, Bowman was scruffy and unshaven. His long brown hair hung straight to his shoulders. A folded blue handkerchief dissected his forehead and flattened his hair just above the ears. His skin was thin and pasty under a hard red sunburn, his eyes hollow and dark.

All in all, he looked like an ex-athlete who had turned hippie and now, twenty years later, was caught up in drugs—running down a steep and narrow path, maybe dealing, maybe smuggling. It was true. All but the last part.

He had played football through high school, even been offered a college scholarship. An injury early in his senior season led the school to revoke the offer.

He'd gone to Kent State instead, enrolling in 1970, just in time to watch the National Guard snap off a few rounds into a crowd of students. That pushed him into The Movement, and it was a long time before he came up for air. But he'd given up the drugs years ago—unless you counted the tequila and the beer, which he did, though he kept drinking them anyway. And The Movement . . . well, it had just grown old and faded away.

Bowman was clean, but that didn't stop the tension from creeping up his neck as he walked toward the border crossing. Gringo Pass. A thin gap in the low hills of the Puerto Blanco Mountains. A hard, hot place with nothing but this official portal between two countries to keep it going.

Bowman tried to remember the last time he had passed a border station unmolested, the way the anglo families in their campers and station wagons were waved through, shooting back home after a weekend at Puerto Peñasco—the rocky point high on the Gulf of California that provided the closest ocean retreat for the worker ants in the air-conditioned steel-and-glass cities of Arizona. He couldn't remember. Maybe never.

Now Bowman felt an additional chisel chipping at the thin rock wall around his nerves. Somewhere back in the desert, near the *tinajas,* was the body of the photographer. And Bowman was still trying to understand why he lay there, lifeless, probably picked mostly clean by now.

He was stunned, shaken and angry. But he wasn't ready to start asking any questions. Not on this side of the border.

He and the photographer had crossed into Mexico together, and they had been traveling down here for more than a week, most of the time on foot. If the body had been found, and if anybody had cared enough to begin investigating—two big ifs along the border—Bowman would be the first one they would want to hold for interrogation.

And the last place Bowman wanted to be right now was in a Mexican jail.

Crossing the border would be dangerous. But on this side of the line, he was an alien, and if he was right about what he had seen at the *tinajas,* landing in a Mexican jail right now could be fatal.

Four

It's just a white line painted on black asphalt,
Bowman wrote. *A line so thin it is almost*
imaginary, a phantom thread cutting through the
thick real blackness, the heat shimmering above it
in syrupy waves.

The crossing was just an arbitrary spot where two very different roads met head on. As Bowman approached it, he saw that there was no traffic on the road out of Mexico, but dozens of Mexicans stood waiting to return home. The bureaucrats were busy today. That was okay with him.

On the right side of the road there was a low, two-room adobe building with a tile-roofed porch over the sidewalk in front of it. Mexican citizens stood in the dark shadow of the porch, forming a line that stretched out of the shade and around the corner of the building.

They funneled into the first room to wait. One at a time they were allowed into the second room, where a man in blue polyester pants and a white shirt would check, then approve or reject their papers. There was always a big show of authority. And a long wait.

In the middle of the road stood a small, shabby, windowed booth, usually manned by one or two young Mexican immigration officers in their bright blue coats.

But today the booth was empty and three uniformed soldiers stood outside of it. Facing them were two men in street clothes—suits and ties—each with a large stomach and one with a thin mustache. The mustache was orating, giving instructions with a flurry of gestures. The young soldiers stood stiffly, paying careful attention.

Bowman stayed on the dirt sidewalk, trudging with his backpack toward the building. He stepped in under the overhang. The shade blinded him. The men and women in line were a long, dark shadow to him, moving gently, arrhythmically from side to side, twisting slowly like a snake stretching after sleep. Children moved in and out, their rustling noises and shrill voices reaching up to Bowman, wrapping around him, encircling his neck, his ears, and the back of his head like the hard, dry-skinned arms of a farm girl.

Out of the corner of his eye Bowman could see that the suits had finished talking to the soldiers. He was looking ahead now, trying to wade through the darkness to the harsh light at the end of the *ramada*. He moved carefully, like a man at a crowded party, a party of strangers, working his way back to the front door; he has found nobody here, none of his friends have come.

The backpack was bulky and awkward, making movement difficult for him. He felt a hand grip his right leg, squeezing his pants pocket in a tight bunch. Bowman lurched back on his good leg, about to jerk away, and the child swung past him laughing, the noise crashing up at him, then was gone. Two more brushed past, taking up the chase.

The suits were walking toward the building, and Bowman tried to move faster.

"*Perdón. Perdón. Perdóname,*" he said quietly, attempting to squeeze by the line, the pack like a horrible appendage on his back, a hump on his shoulder inescapable even here, even in the darkness. Now he was beyond the doorway, and the line thinned and stretched. He stepped to the inside of the ramada, hugging the wall, keeping a human buffer between himself and the Mexican police.

Two children, small, not four and five yet. They knelt on the cement sidewalk at their parents' feet, playing with some toy. Bowman could see the shape of them clearly, silhouetted against the gathering light beyond, but he could not see what they played. He slowed, moving gently, taking a high, careful step over them. The pain built quickly in his knee like a child's pent-up rage, then shrieked up his leg. He buckled at the waist, caught himself, and kept going.

Behind him a man was pushing his way out of the building through the thick knot of people. The man was calling to the suits.

"*Allí! Allí!*" He pointed at Bowman. The suits stared into the darkness, trying to see.

Bowman moved faster now, bumping roughly past the people in line. He broke from the darkness into harsh sunlight. The fence was just ahead.

Two choices. To the right, a sidewalk ran through a small gate and down a long, fenced corridor. On the left was the roadway—two open lanes, no traffic. The sidewalk was a little closer, but Bowman jogged left, cutting onto the road. On the sidewalk, there was no white line.

Five

Bowman lumbered up the road, eyes locked on the borderline. The soldiers and the suits were after him. They were running. Bowman looked back once and broke for it, banging away at an ugly sprint with all he had left.

His legs felt weak, rubbery. His right leg was stiff, and he was shocked with pain by each step.

A soft October night. High school. A football game. Bowman had played every minute of the first three quarters. Midway through the fourth quarter, the play called for him to go out on a fly pattern. He flashed past his man, caught the pass on his fingertips and ran straight over the defensive safety. He rushed up the field, watching markers flash under him: 50, 45, 40, 35, 30. . . .

Then his legs quit. He never really knew how it happened. They just stopped. Like the nightmare slow motion of an accident, he simply wound down. He fell flat, his chin strap digging into the grass. Then there was the hit. A helmet digging into his back and the *pop-pop,* like the echo of a distant rifle shot but coming from inside somewhere, ending his season, changing his future.

Now it was happening again. His legs were going slack. Suddenly he was just too tired to walk another step, and that same nightmare of helpless falling flashed through his mind. It seemed that he was disconnected from his body.

Bowman reached out frantically with his right hand. His fingers raked down the chain link of the border fence, twanging a soft, sick riff on the hard wire. Then they caught. Fingers like claws, he hooked onto the fence, swinging on one arm, shifting weight, using momentum to pull himself upright.

He looked back over his shoulder. The soldiers were close, the suits a few steps behind. He moved.

Then he was at the line. One step, then over.

Two customs agents, one tall and thin, the other short and blocky, ran from the small building on the American side, hands on pistols, side by side in a careful trot.

Bowman didn't like customs agents much. These were the guys who searched his pack every time he returned home, jogging their big sloppy German shepherd out to sniff through his clothes and his first-aid kit. He was happy to see them now.

He staggered a few more steps into the United States.

The Mexican soldiers had stopped at the line. They stood in a short row, automatic rifles slung under their arms and pointed at the ground, half-ready, fingers on triggers.

Bowman shuffled a few more steps north. He smiled his thin smile and leaned back against the chain link. Bad leg and all, he had won this little footrace.

Then the mustache pushed past the soldiers, his partner following. The mustache stepped across the white line. He was panting hard, his huge stomach jerking up and down with each gasp. He put one hand out and paused to catch his breath. Then he spoke.

"Señor," he said, "you are under arrest."

Six

The customs agents had slowed to a cautious walk. Bowman turned and looked their way. The short one had unsnapped his holster, freeing his gun to draw. The other was thumbing the shiny snap on his holster uncertainly.

"American citizen," Bowman said to them. "I have my passport."

Now the suits were on him. The mustache raised a badge high over his head.

"This one is our prisoner," he said. *"No es suyo."*

His partner looked worried. He sought the mustache's eyes for reassurance. The mustache ignored him. He worked his way carefully between Bowman and the customs officers.

"This man is under arrest," The mustache spoke easily, softly, in a lilting Mexican accent, putting on a precise show of how casual it all was. He gestured in a matter-of-fact way at Bowman, as if explaining a truth everybody present already knew.

"He is a murderer. He is under arrest for the murder of a citizen of Mexico."

The mustache began to ease backward, pushing Bowman south toward the line. "He is in my custody."

Bowman had no more strength. He felt his legs go rubbery again. His mind screamed. With bleary eyes, he looked at the customs agents. He knew that once he was back on the Mexican side, things would fall apart, the center would not hold, and events would simply spin out of control around him, finally taking his life.

The short one spoke, his gun half-unholstered.

"You've crossed the line," he said to the mustache. "You're out of your jurisdiction."

The mustache backed away another step, pocketing his badge.

"No," he said. "He will come with us. He does not want to stay here." He was pushing Bowman along easily now. Bowman's will to resist was gone. He slumped into the mustache. The mustache held him up by one arm.

"You see. He wants to return with us."

Bowman struggled with himself, willing the strength to move, digging deep through dehydrated exhaustion, spurring himself with fear. The mustache held him up effortlessly, pulling him against his quivering belly. The fat cop moved his bulk well, and it felt like most of the stomach was thick muscle.

Bowman twisted, trying to pull away from the man and lunge north. The grip on his arm was unbreakable, made of stone.

Bowman closed his eyes and concentrated, preparing to give it one last try. He took a deep breath, dipped his shoulder, and dropped the backpack from his free arm. Then he swung the pack around and let its lumpy weight fall on the mustache's wrist. At the same time, he pivoted on his good leg, breaking away and diving to the ground.

The mustache grunted, his grip broken, fingers twisting under the weight of the pack.

The short customs agent bolted forward, stepping toward Bowman and the mustache.

One of the *Federales* raised his rifle in a quick aim at the American agent. The other suit swung hard at him, knocking the rifle up in the air. The shot was like a hard slap, echoing off the canyon walls in receding waves of stinging pain. There was a frozen moment. Then everyone was moving at once.

The short customs man dropped to the ground, scrambling for cover behind the backpack. His partner stood, shoulders hunched, looking madly back and forth for the nearest cover, like a surreal animated statue, fixed eternally in a crazed pattern of indecision.

Bowman crawled on his belly, squirming north, away from the border.

Then the Mexican soldiers were yelling and scrambling backward into their country, the suits hustling behind them.

The short customs guard had his gun out now, and he balanced it on top of Bowman's pack and lay there panting.

Seven

It took a long time. But slowly Bowman eased his way through the interrogation. Answering the same questions again and again, refusing to alter his responses, clear and simple, and sounding perhaps just a little bit stupid. He sat in a small room, its walls painted an aggravating color of pink, and spoke into the microphone of a tape recorder that sat on the metal table in front of him.

He performed the act repeatedly, until even to his interrogators, it got boring. Still, he plodded on, setting one answer down after the other, trudging slowly across a desert of bureaucratic questions.

The two men asking the questions were big and rough-looking but dressed in suits, not in uniforms. They had introduced themselves as Agents Crawford and Mails, of the Justice Department.

"What were you doing out there, Mister Bowman?" Crawford asked again. Mails sat quietly, his feet kicked up on the table. His legs, crossed at the ankles, flexed every few minutes, pushing the chair backward until it bumped against the wall. Then he would rock forward a little and hover until the next time.

"Just crossing the border," Bowman said.

"I heard you the first time. But what were you *doing*? What got them after you?"

"I've never seen those men in my life."

"Have you ever been arrested before, either here or abroad, Mister Bowman?"

"No . . . well, once when I was a teenager. For disturbing the peace," Bowman said. Then, with an easy grin, "But I didn't do it."

Mails jerked his feet off the table, slamming the chair to its upright position.

"You know, you're pretty much of a smart-ass punk," he said. It wasn't a question.

The smile disappeared from Bowman's face. "I'm aware of that, yeah."

"Maybe you don't understand just how unfunny you really are," Mails continued. "Or how much trouble you can make for yourself right here in this little room. Maybe you think it doesn't matter when we get shot at by the other side. You know—"

Crawford cut him off. "What's your occupation, Bowman?"

"Occupation?" Bowman thought about it for a moment. Scout? Walker? Adventurer? Fool? All of them were suitable, to a point, but none seemed to fit perfectly. Finally he settled for the old standby.

"I'm a journalist."

He gave them the name of his paper, as well as his editor's name and phone number in Tucson. "Check it out for yourselves if you want," he said.

There was more. He told them of how he had come down here to write a story on a desert trail that had been traveled for hundreds, maybe thousands, of years, and of how he had intended to walk through the barren ground on that waterless trail and come to terms with the desert's anger, or be broken by it.

He explained about walking to the *tinajas* in search of tepid little pools of dirty water. He told them of thirst that devoured hunger and made it impossible to eat from the little packets of dehydrated food in his backpack.

He told them of how he had found no water on the pitted mesa atop the *tinajas,* and of how he had fallen on the way down, then walked out of the desert, broken by the hard dryness, hallucinating from exhaustion and dehydration.

Each time he told them the same things, the same way, keeping it simple and direct. And each time he left out the same details. He did not tell them about the night, about scrambling up the rock in the dark under a moonless sky, about the small group of men with bags—not backpacks, but big duffels that zip down the middle and can be slung under one arm. He did not tell them about the faces he saw in the flashlight beams, or about the rounds of film that had been snapped off silently in the night, or about the guns. He did not tell them about the photographer.

Crawford stepped out of the room for a while, leaving Bowman to sit in silence with Mails. When he returned, he had an official-looking piece of paper with handwriting scrawled across it.

"We checked with Allen Bauldaff at *The Weekly,*" Crawford said.

Bowman nodded.

"He vouched for you. Said you have business down here. He wants us to ease up a little. You're lucky. He knows people.

"But you know, Bowman, we're not going to list you among our journalist friends."

"Of which you have none," Bowman said.

"That's right," Mails said, slamming his chair to the floor again. "And it's nice every once in a while to meet an asshole like you. It convinces us we're doing the right thing. I don't know who you killed in Mexico, but we don't appreciate your getting us shot at. If we had anything to hold you on, you can bet we would."

They told him they might have more questions, and asked where they could reach him. He was glad to tell them; he would be safely hunched over his computer back at *The Weekly*'s offices just as soon as he could get there.

Outside, he felt lousy. Empty, exhausted, and rotten. Lying hadn't bothered him. But the shooting in the desert had left him feeling wasted.

The photographer, who had always seemed so much a part of this rough region—like the mesquite, the creosote, the lava rock—had simply been eliminated, truncated, rubbed out.

And Bowman knew that the only way to make up for it was to find out who had killed Vyking, and expose them.

To do that, he would have to go back to the city.

His vehicle was where he'd left it, outside the Gringo Pass Cafe. The left rear tire of the battered old Land Cruiser was considerably lower than when he parked it.

But his arrangement with the fat man who ran the little grocery store and greasy spoon across the street from the border station—a few dollars to have the boxy four-wheel drive watched—didn't include service.

Somewhere under the layers of dust, dirt, and mud that covered the vehicle there was a faded, forest-green paint job that showed through clearly only after the occasional hard rainfall. Bowman had not washed the Land Cruiser since he bought it, years before.

It was old and ugly, and it had a large hole in the muffler, which, as a result, no longer muffled. When driven, the car bleated like a baritone sheep. It was a 1967 model, with a column shift and a straight-six motor; its top speed was somewhere around sixty-five miles per, unless you wanted a new set of valves every ten thousand miles. But the Land Cruiser took him to the places where the roads ended and the thin jeep tracks began, and then farther, to where even those trails vanished and only desert and mountains lay beyond. There, where the scrub brush took over, he would park—just stop and cut the engine. Then he would walk. The vehicle took him that far each time. And it had never failed to get him back out again.

Bowman topped the tank and filled the tire with air, then he used the gas-station pay phone to call Allen.

"Nate! Jesus, are you all right? I've been on the phone for hours trying to get you out of there."

"I'm okay now. And thanks," Bowman said. "I've got something here, Al, something big. Complete with photos. Save me the front page. But there's bad news . . ."

"John," the editor said. "Is John okay?"

Bowman was quiet. Finally the editor spoke.

"Right, Nate. I have something on the stove for you here, too. Just come on back, and we'll sort it out at this end."

"I'm on the road now. Be there in a few hours."

"Right," the editor said again, and with a click, he was gone.

Bowman paid for his gas, and with the Land Cruiser emitting an extended staccato belch, he hit the desert road. Smoother on this side, with less trash on the shoulders. The asphalt sliced a singular symmetrical swath through the rough landscape. Soon he turned right, heading for home.

Eight

Bowman crested the gap at Gates Pass and wound down the steep, curving road toward town.

Tucson lay before him like a sequined gown thrown in a hump with the laundry. Twinkling lights coated the twisting, bumpy floor of the valley, and at the far end, tucked against the mountains, unseen in the darkness, the smelter at the Apricot Mine coughed black smoke skyward.

By a twist of fate that Bowman found not at all amusing, the prevailing weather pattern in the valley blew the Apricot's smoke through a gap in the hills and into the next valley. In the last few years, management at the mine had gotten smart about public image and begun releasing waste through the smokestacks only late at night, when it was all but invisible. As a result, the people of the pueblo couldn't, or didn't, see the damage being done year after year as the mine refined its ore and leached its pollution into the atmosphere. The only way to see the destruction was by driving an old jeep trail through a gap in the mountains called Redington Pass to the smoggy agricultural valley on the other side, and the giant tailings ponds. Ponds! Bowman thought, another euphemism. Toxic dumps was what they were, and they were slowly leaking down into the ground, killing the waters hidden there.

The San Pedro Valley was being poisoned to death, and the only ones who knew about it were a handful of ranchers, a few fanatic conservationists, and a small group of thoroughly corrupt mine owners.

The mountains rose in the blackening twilight like the Dark Man in a children's cartoon, mean and foreboding, sharp crags of stone shooting skyward.

Now the lights took on distinct forms and became landmarks. There were the Twin Towers—North and South—conical, troposphere-tickling giants that thundered up from the desert floor like hunched weightlifters. There was the money. It flowed toward the Towers as if by force of nature.

Unseen beyond the Towers, tucked against a tall brick building, was an old, slowly crumbling adobe villa—home of *The Weekly*. The building's white paint was veined with thin cracks, and the frames of all the windows seemed slightly ajar, as if some giant had picked the place up like a bag of cubed ice and thumped it on the ground. But the big wooden doors of the courtyard led to the home of the one consistent voice of truth in the wild western town, where newspapers, like water rights, were for sale to the highest bidder.

And off to the left lay a spread of red brick and green grass: the University of Arizona, mostly dark now in the summer night, even the massive cement oval of the football stadium lifeless.

Bowman cut the wheel hard, pulling through the final, sharp curve at the bottom of the pass.

Before him lay the wide bed of the Santa Cruz, a desert river that once flowed year-round and flooded nearly a mile wide. Now it was a dry scar at the city's edge. He crossed the bridge and plunged into the pool of lights.

Nine

The room was stuffy and the crowd spilled out past the heavy metal doors into the summer night. Dark silhouetted shapes blocked Bowman's view.

Hunched low over a long table at the front of the room, the members of the City Council sat under the glaring lights like frightened gnomes, shying away from angry glares in the crowd.

A fat man in an expensive gray suit addressed the Council from a lectern. His face was red, his nose veined in thin, dark lines. His voice was a honk, and when he spoke, his jowls bounced loosely up and down.

"This," he said, "is much ado about nothing. These protestations, these demonstrations, these remonstrations, mean nothing. It is nothing. You could stick them all with a pin, and pin them, wriggling, to the wall. Why, then, do we waste our time?"

He stepped from behind the lectern. For all his bulk, he moved with ease in the sprightly, careful step of a dancer.

"Why are we here?" He approached the low banister—the railing that separated Council from audience—and leaned forward with his arms spread out. For a moment it looked as though he might take the whole huddled bunch of them in a warm hug, lifting them onto his lap, where they could rest safe and secure, his hands at their backs like a ventriloquist's.

"We are here because the special interests, the vocal minority, the loud but powerless coalitions, have decided to raise a fuss," he said with the patient grimace of a mother describing her youngest child, the one who *refuses* to give up diapers for potty training.

There was movement, a deep rustling in the audience. Led by a man in ragged jeans and river sandals, voices rose in opposition.

The fat man silenced them with a challenging look beneath his great arched brow.

"We are here because a small band of *neighbors,* no less guilty than street criminals—" he spat out the word "neighbors" as if it were burning his mouth—"has decided to lie down on the tracks of progress. The tracks of *dreams.*

"And do you know where those tracks lead? Those tracks lead to the future. And we can't afford to slow down or to move these criminals out of harm's way. Because the future is ours. The future is jobs and lower taxes and better opportunity for our children and their children. The future is bright, and I want to go there. We must take back these streets."

Again, the audience rumbled. Bowman recognized the leader of the protest group as a local architect—one of the growing number of neighborhood activists possessed of a zealous certainty that the fat man must be stopped, that if he weren't, he would destroy their community. For a moment it looked as if the group might rise up in insurrection and overthrow the Council, taking the meeting into their own righteous hands.

Again the fat man quieted them with a withering look, one that said *Will you prove me right?*

Favoring his bad leg, Bowman worked his way across the back of the room and down the narrow aisle along one wall.

From the look of things, this was going to be an interesting meeting. Bowman almost hadn't come inside.

Having stopped at home to shower, change clothes, and unload his vehicle, he had taken time to clean and dress the cut on his knee as well. It didn't look so bad, really, and the swelling had started to ease.

Then, on his way out the door, he had knelt down on the wooden slats of his front porch. The adobe bricks along the bottom of his old house were visible through battered coats of paint and stucco. One of the bricks was loose—loose enough to be pulled out, and behind it was a space Bowman had hollowed out with a screwdriver. At times he had left a house key there for one woman or another—when they'd reached the point where things had gotten close enough, but not too far.

He'd taken the film cartridge from his pocket, wadded it up in a blue bandana, and stuffed it back into the recess, then replaced the brick.

After that he'd driven downtown.

He'd headed for the Weekly Building, expecting to find the business district quiet, the parking lots empty. But *The Weekly*'s lot was full, and down at the end of the street, noise and light had been pouring out of City Hall into the summer night.

He was still shaken by the events in Mexico. How could John be dead? What the hell had happened out there along the *camino?*

A shower and food had taken the edge off of his exhaustion. He felt a little more human and was anxious to get to work. He wanted to talk to Allen and the other editors, to get them on the phone to *The Weekly*'s lawyer, and eventually to the Justice Department.

But he had been compelled by curiosity to find out where in the hell all these cars had come from, and what all these people were doing at night downtown, usually the haunt of transients, college students, and a few, like Bowman, who were somewhere in between.

He had driven around the block twice looking for a parking place and finally cut down an alley, squeezing the big four-wheel drive illegally between two dumpsters.

He'd wondered what the ruckus could be about, and then he had realized it was July twenty-first. He had been in Mexico for almost two weeks, which made this the third Wednesday of the month. Voting night for the City Council.

Now, from his vantage point, squeezed back in the shadows by the railing, he watched both crowd and Council. The fat man preened before both, feeling all eyes upon him.

It was, Bowman realized, an old story, one that had been around in different incarnations longer than most people imagined. Development versus conservation. Pro growth versus no growth.

As far as Bowman was concerned, it had started long before his time. It had started, in fact, before any white man set foot in the territory.

On a warm spring day in 1536, a Spaniard named Alvar Nuñez Cabeza de Vaca had stumbled into a clearing not too far south of the room Bowman was now working his way carefully around, and startled the hell out of a couple of conquistadors on horseback. Cabeza de Vaca and his three companions—the only survivors of a group stranded in what would become Florida—had been walking for eight years across the continent and were wandering around in Bowman's Sonoran desert.

The conquistadors who found Cabeza de Vaca's group were happily surprised. They'd just about finished raping and pillaging the lands to the south. The survival of Cabeza de Vaca's group represented to them the opportunity of new places to plunder in the uncharted north.

Cabeza de Vaca objected. Once a conquistador himself, he had found spirituality out there in the wilderness among the "savages." He thought the People and the land deserved a little more respect.

Thus had begun a conflict that after four hundred years was no closer to being settled. The *cantores* had changed, but the *canción* remained the same.

Now, instead of conquistadors, there were rich and greedy developers who wanted to tear away chunks of freedom and sell it off one parcel at a time. The people were neighborhood activists who had moved to the great southwest when it was still great, and had begun to feel all that wide-open space slipping away from them.

The problem was simple. Everyone who came here wanted to be the last one in. Bowman's friend Edward Abbey, Cactus Ed, the southwest's great writer, put it best. "It's a beautiful place," he said. "Don't go there."

The fat man was Porter Eisor, attorney at law, representative of various local land developers and investors—Though Bowman privately wondered how anyone could think of it as "developing" the land when they scraped off its vastly intricate, naturally formed face and replaced it with poorly constructed, aesthetically inferior block houses, complete with imported shrubs and green grass lawns.

It was like doing massive reconstructive surgery—the kind that leaves the patient looking like a blob of badly formed rubber with two beady eyes—on a beautiful patient who has not been in an accident. It was, Bowman thought, like doing a touch-up on a Van Gogh.

Eisor was the defender of the realm. The lead salesman. One of the most powerful men in town. It was said that the man had political dirt on every significant player in the game. It was also said that Eisor had started out working for the developers, but that they now worked for him, and that he had made more money and buried more bodies than any other lawyer in the southwest. But it was said quietly, and never when it might be overheard by the wrong people.

Currently, Eisor was defending the right of a wealthy gentleman named Dino Diamante, who, along with a small syndicate, wanted to "develop" a place they hoped to buy called Puma Canyon, at the base of the Coronado National Forest along the Santa Catalina Range—the mountains that formed one crooked arm against which Tucson nestled.

Eisor's client planned to put four golf courses and three international hotels in a half-circle at the foot of the canyon. The project would close the canyon to the public and reduce the water supply from the riparian area's stream to a trickle, starving out ranchers in valleys on the public lands to the north.

Thousands of the city's three-quarter-million population vehemently opposed the development. It wasn't that there weren't other canyons to hike. Or that they cared all that much about what happened to a handful of crusty old ranchers.

They were just tired. They had seen enough. They wanted to be the last ones in. The door, they thought, should be closed behind them. And the City Council had the power to do just that, having acquired control of the canyon through a land swap with the BLM.

But the developers could match the activists, a hundred, a thousand dollars to the head. And when that kind of money talked, the Council listened. And rolled over. And begged.

Bowman had been following the controversy carefully, and had written about it in *The Weekly.*

"My client has tried to come to terms with these people," the fat man bellowed, "though they would destroy him for what he is. For his fair complexion, his clothing, neat and clean, and my Lord, he even wears a necktie. But not in their neighborhood. Let him move somewhere else. Let him try to build his future in another town, another neighborhood."

Now he affected a hayseed accent. "Just keep movin' down the road, buddy, we don't want any of your kind here. And you don't want a little trouble, do you? A little help to the county line?"

Eisor moved gracefully around the podium. At the table

next to him sat a young woman with wild black hair, sharp features, and dark brown eyes. As the fat man moved behind her, gesticulating with his stumpy arms, he brushed his enormous belly against her back.

"My client has made this venture nearly unprofitable to himself by acquiescing to the demands of this ragtag band of unruly toughs. He has made concessions, though the law says he does not have to do so. Why? Because he is a good neighbor and willing to prove it. And what is he told, wherefore comes the answer?" Again he spoke with the hick twang. "No room, mistah. Just keep movin'.'"

The architect, his thick beard trembling with rage, shot out of his seat. "Filth! Filth!" He shouted.

Bowman tried to remember the man's name, and he had to laugh when it came to him. Alexander Paz. Paz was looking anything but peaceful at the moment. He had in his eye the challenging look of a man for whom an important debate has come down to a single point. But when he opened his mouth it seemed he could express it in only a single word.

"Filthy, filthy, *filthy!*" He sputtered with rage.

Eisor turned with a chilling look. Two burly men dressed in suits appeared at the back of the room. They moved quickly down the aisle and grabbed the architect roughly by the shoulders, yanking him from his place and hustling him away.

The architect struggled, but one of the guards slapped a hand hard against the side of his neck and squeezed. It worked. The architect turned white and shaky and gave no more resistance as he was dragged up the crowded aisle.

The fat man shrugged gently as the protester was pulled out into the night. He turned back to the Council, asking their permission to continue. He was met with meek nods.

The crowd, however, was not silenced this time. Its restless anger was building.

It was gathering force and energy, surging forward, then ebbing like a huge, horrible creature trapped and breathing deeply in the stuffy room. Nobody sat. All were in front of their chairs, many jeering, and more of them seemed to keep pushing in through the twin double doors.

Bowman sat by the low railing. It formed a barrier more imaginary than real, a thin wooden line protecting the governors from the governed. To Bowman, as the crowd cat-called and glowered, it looked as if that line was being stretched ever thinner. It looked, in fact, as if it might well snap at any moment.

He glanced over his left shoulder. A few feet of the Council side of the railing there was a wide door. The rectangular sign above it said "Exit" in red neon. The push-bar across the door latched into a box at one end with more red lettering; "Emergency Exit Only. Alarm Will Sound."

Even if things really went to hell, Bowman figured his chances of getting out quick were pretty good. Not that he actually thought it would go that far. This angry group would probably just break up and drift off, taking their frustrations with them and turning them on spouses and pets, strangers at the bar, or the idiot in the car just ahead on the drive home. But crowds made Bowman uneasy. They always had.

He preferred the huge, rough emptiness of the desert. Bowman would take a crowd of saguaros over a group of humans any day. The saguaros might drink more, but they wouldn't put you out of chips-and-dip and then riot in your front yard when you ran out of beer. There was something in the stoic demeanor of the gigantic cactus that bespoke a spirit of whole and deliberate, thoughtful peace—as if the saguaros had reached an understanding in their thick, fleshy meat that man could not begin to approach. So they sat, and they waited. It seemed like it to Bowman, anyway.

"We few," the fat man was saying, "we proud few have opposed them, and so ended their grip on our future. We have cut the ties that bind and found it feels good, it feels *good* to be free. We have found that we are *good* people, *good* neighbors, and we *welcome* this man. If he wants to develop, then, like a healthy young woman—" and here he turned to the dark woman, whom he favored with a big, leering wink—"let him develop."

There was a rustling at the back of the room. A few yelps, a terrified scream, and the crowd surged forward. Bowman eased toward the door, ready to plunge out of the room, which suddenly seemed to take on all the aspects of a tight little box of matches baking in the desert sun.

There were more shouts of surprise, and a young couple in the front row clambered over the low wooden rail. A cop appeared suddenly, and behind him, two more of the plain-clothes security guards. They moved in on the couple, who had stopped just inside the railing and were looking around with confused faces, unsure of how to proceed. It was as if the young man and his . . . what? Bowman thought. Wife? Girlfriend? Lover, anyway, were caught in an invisible force field of authority that surrounded the Council members in their seats.

The security guards, part of Eisor's private force, meant business. But the cop was short and lumpy, with pinkish cheeks that huffed as he rushed headlong into the fray, a sloppy, betraying grin on his face. The adrenaline buzz had turned his eyeballs milky and unseeing, and he looked for all the world like a badly overweight, alcoholic shark arcing in on wounded prey.

"My goddamnit," he panted under his labored breath. "Looks like we get to kick some shit toni—"

He caught up short as the pointed horns of the first steer poked through the crowd, which was parting now like arroyo brush in a flash flood, bending away from the massive force suddenly upon it.

Ten

There was only one bull, and that was good, Bowman thought. The horns of a sufficiently enraged bull were nasty weapons that could maim, even kill. Whoever was pulling this stunt was taking a big chance that nobody would get hurt. Or else didn't care.

A herd of ten or twelve cattle followed, pushing through the open double doors and milling down the wide aisle. Chairs were knocked over and trampled. People crowded back and the exits popped open. Cool air rushed out into the night and the first panicked individuals clambered after it.

The Council members, along with the mayor and a rather harried-looking stenographer, bolted from their seats and rushed out the door behind them, into private chambers. They were followed by the fat cop, who stumbled after them with a crazed look on his face and sweat pouring down his pink cheeks.

Eisor and the brunette ducked out a side exit, where they were led away in quick, efficient movements by the bodyguards.

Bowman moved to the exit, then stepped past it, circling around behind the Council seats, now empty, to take a final look at the room. Straight out of *Chinatown,* he thought, and it brought a smile to his face.

There were shrieks from the crowd and the cattle lowed.

A skinny man in blue jeans and a ratty T-shirt fainted dead away in the third row and was pulled out of the fray by a tall, thick-shouldered *vaquero* in a straw hat.

A stout woman in a dirty sundress stood stubbornly in the aisle, banging her hip into the bodies of the cattle as they shouldered past her. Bowman marveled at the force she mustered. As each cow came abreast of her, she would rock back, then swing her massive flank into it, shifting the animal visibly in its path, keeping it moving straight down the aisle.

Another woman shrank under her chair and whimpered, but the *vaqueros* pushed their way over to her and helped her out of the room.

Now Bowman could see two men at the back of the herd maneuvering the cattle forward by snapping ropes at their flanks. Under their hats they wore bandannas masking their faces like stagecoach robbers in an old western.

The cattle crashed through the small fence and rumbled among the Council's chairs and table, knocking them over. Then the dumb, big-eyed animals paused. (Seldom Seen Smith had called them "slow elk," Bowman suddenly remembered.) Apparently satisfied that they had found a roomy corral, the cattle stalled, waiting for further direction. A man worked his way up from the back of the thinning crowd as the herd was being corralled. When he got near, he grabbed Bowman's shoulder, crumpling the shirt in his big, hairy hand.

"Mister Bowman?"

"I don't know you," Bowman said, looking at the man's hand and then around the room. The world had truly gone crazy.

The man was short and blocky, with big muscles under his tailored suit, his hair slicked back and knotted in a ponytail.

"Mister Bowman, I have a message for you. From a local developer."

"My phone number's in the book," Bowman said. "Tell your boss to call me himself." He grabbed the meaty hand and wrenched it loose by the thumb.

From the look on the goon's face, he was surprised at Bowman's strength.

"I'm supposed to give it to you now," the goon said, staring at his hand with a look of confusion, as if wondering what to do with it next. Finally he shoved it into his coat pocket. "The message is this: there are many sides to every story. He thinks you're being one-sided about things lately. Maybe too one-sided."

"Thanks. I'm always happy to hear from my fans," Bowman said, turning away.

"Hey, Bowman," the man called after him. "Are you afraid of things that go bump in the night?" Bowman looked back. "Maybe you should be." Then the goon disappeared into the crowd.

Bowman headed for the exit, anxious to put some distance between himself and the little man, with his meaty hands and his slick, MTV hair.

As he ducked through the doorway, Bowman paused to look back one last time. The goon was nowhere to be seen.

The masked men were working their way around the cattle, apparently getting ready to herd them back up the aisle.

Watching the chaos, Bowman had time for a final thought. The thirteen head of cattle were probably worth five thousand dollars each. That was more than your average rancher could afford to lose to police impoundment for the dubious honor of making a political statement.

Who, Bowman wondered, paid for all that beef?

Eleven

Bowman. *Bowman!*" The woman's voice echoed down the breezeway.

He thought about ignoring her. He could duck into the shadows, cut under an archway and take a slightly longer route around the Towers, avoiding confrontation and escaping into the swamp-cooled darkness of *The Weekly*'s offices.

"Goddamnit, Bowman, I'll hunt you down and kill you."

He stopped, waiting for the *clop-clop* of high-heeled shoes to catch up with him. Probably she wouldn't make good on the threat. But Bowman knew her well enough not to lay down the gauntlet. He turned to face her.

Under the phosphorescent lights, her black hair was a shimmering blue. Her dark eyes, veiled in shadows, reminded Bowman of corny lines in old novels about Spanish eyes that flashed with black fire.

"Hello, Theresa," Bowman said.

"Did you have anything to do with that?" Her tone was accusing, and he figured the question was already answered in her mind.

He looked her over. Theresa Saldivar. Thirty-six years

old. A native of the desert city who, other than a year spent studying at a Mexican university, had never left home.

In the first two years out of law school, she'd worked as a public defender. It was why she had endured three grinding years of law school in the first place, to defend the disenfranchised poor.

But before long she had started to have creeping doubts about her work. Did she really want to keep criminals out of jail? Few of her clients had been falsely accused. None had been innocent. Doubt turned to certainty, and finally to cynicism.

She went back to school for a year, concentrating on tax and realty law, then spent a year at U.N.A.M. in Mexico City. When she returned home, she was hired onto Porter Eisor's staff.

She was the fat man's first minority and only female attorney, and she ascended quickly. Cynicism turned into Machiavellian skill, and she became certain that she had made the right move.

Bowman often wondered how she could put up with Eisor's innuendos, his horrible stomach at her back, the fat man brushing against her like a leering buffalo. The question, however, resided in an area that was on the other side of some unseen line. So Bowman left it alone.

He considered her question, thought about ignoring it.

"I've been out of town," he said finally.

"How long?"

"A while. I've been working."

"I'm sure you have. Where have you been?"

"Your line of questioning is getting tiresome, Counselor. You want to get to the point?"

"Our project has been under attack from the start, Bowman, and these little stunts are growing more frequent. And more extreme." Her dark eyes flashed. She was angry.

Bowman felt a stirring inside. Her energy was attractive.

"Cattle. You call cattle extreme?"

"That's just a small part of it. The monkey-wrenching has been going on in private, too. Homesites vandalized, equipment destroyed. In the dark. When nobody's around. No witnesses, Bowman, just like goon squads down south. Isn't that the way they operate?"

"Shooting tractors is a little different than shooting children."

"A higher moral cause makes it okay, right?"

He said nothing.

"I read your last story," she continued. "The big, mean developer is kicking the poor old family off its homestead, going to shut off access to a little patch of desert scrub to a raggedy group of unbathed naturalists.

"But you leave out the inconvenient details. Like the little old lady spent twelve years in jail for killing her husband. And the land doesn't belong to her anymore. Our client bought it. Even when the little old lady owned it, she'd just as soon shoot the shrub-huggers as let them on her land. And now the construction company has to deal with threats and vandalism on a daily basis."

"Damn, that's a sad story."

Bowman had left out some of those details. Only because they weren't relevant. The woman had indeed been convicted of killing her husband—in 1947. And she hadn't at first freely allowed visitors, but in more recent years, hikers could cross her property without raising her ire. She had sold the land, a fact he had included in the article, but she had also been defrauded by a very slick young attorney with a contract that looked more like a lease than a sale, until you inspected the four-point type. An attorney who happened to work for Porter Eisor.

"It's one you ought to write about in *The Weekly*," she said. "But then again, you seem to have an aversion to the truth."

"This interview is over," he said.

"Fine. But tell me, Nate, do you really understand how serious it's gotten? Two guys disappeared off a site last week."

"Construction workers aren't tied down by BMW payments and Brooks Brothers suits."

"And running a bunch of cattle into the Council meeting isn't going to help anybody," she continued.

"It got the vote put off," Bowman said.

"For a while. Did you know that Eisor's life has been threatened?"

"We all have problems."

Now for the first time she looked at him closely.

"Are you okay?"

"Ugly and tired. The usual."

"Where have you been, Bowman?"

"The border. *Camino del Diablo*. I've been walking the Devil's Highway. You'll read about it in the paper."

She looked more intently into his eyes. "What have you gotten into?"

"I can't talk about it. I'm on my way to the Weekly Building. The Council meeting was just something I stumbled into. I've been doing that a lot lately."

She held his gaze for a moment, probing his face as if she might find might be some clue there. Then she accepted. She understood that there were certain things Bowman just wouldn't talk about. When he started clamming up, she left it alone. But her eyes got sharp.

"There are things going on that you don't understand, Nate."

"That's not unusual."

She seemed to consider saying something more, then she let it go. Her expression softened.

"Are you coming over?" she asked.

"I have to get the story started while it's still fresh. I'm going to the Weekly Building now, and I'll sit in front of a computer screen until I finish it."

She looked around, then pushed him gently back into the shadows. He leaned against the rough surface of one of the huge cylindrical pillars that abutted the Twin Towers. She was disagreeable, cold, and thoroughly brilliant, the last of which made her unattractive to most men. But that intense intelligence was the first thing Bowman liked about her.

He had met her while researching a story on the destruction of a cactus forest by a developer. Professionally, they had never agreed on much. But they'd gotten beyond professions.

"How about later?" she asked, her voice quiet, forceful. It was this fierce will, this fiery determination, that had held his attention for nearly two years.

"Later?" he said.

She shoved him back against the rough surface, pushing her hips hard against his and pressing her breasts to him as she leaned up, seeking his mouth. She kissed him, gently at first; then their lips came together more forcefully and opened up. His tongue slipped inside and explored the familiar terrain of her mouth. She pulled away quickly, still pinning his hips to the wall in a way that left them both a little out of breath.

"Later," he said. She looked at him for a moment, then kissed him again, hard.

"Good-bye, Bowman."

Twelve

In a land of little rain, Bowman wrote, *you can feed golf courses only by starving something else. Tell me how many golf courses you want, and I'll tell you how much of the desert will have to die.*

Theresa. He didn't know when it had happened. But somewhere along the line she had become an indispensable part of his life. Love? He'd given up on that a long time ago. This was something like it, but without the creeping, insidious, viral changes, the metamorphoses people go through after being in love for a while—butterflies turning into caterpillars.

Theresa was the first woman he'd had a relationship with for any length of time who had not simply grown tired of him, quietly packing and leaving.

He'd been married twice. "You're an asshole," his second wife had said as she pulled the door closed after her.

With Theresa, it had started slowly and remained unsteady, but only once had they seriously come close to separation.

It had been more than a year since the Fight. He couldn't even remember anymore how it had started. But the genesis of the thing had quickly become irrelevant as months of pent-up frustrations and slights, imagined and real, had come flooding back in one unholy hour of personal combat.

He remembered only the monster he had become at the end, raging through the small apartment, bellowing his statements of broad condemnation, then pausing to dissect narrowly defined points, backing her into rhetorical corners. "So you're telling me I'm *lying* when I say . . ." And even in the flushed rage, he had listened to his own voice. It reminded him of his father's. And he was horrified.

He'd left then, crashing out of the house, slamming the front door open, then closed, and leaving in his wake the overturned table, a broken coffee mug, the shattered glass of a picture frame.

He'd felt hot and angry, and humiliated by the rage that had taken control of him.

So he'd gone to the desert, and he'd walked. He'd walked for two days along a wide wash beneath the palo verdes and the mesquite, far into the desert country of the O'Odham.

He'd had no food. It was late summer, and in the afternoon, the rain clouds appeared in the south. The dark, boiling thunderheads on the horizon billowed forward on the monsoon winds like special effects in a horror movie.

When the winds came, he'd walked against them, then stopped and finally sat as the rain broke. He soaked in the rain, feeling it pound down on him. While the wash ran, he drank from it, sucking the water through his handkerchief. After the storm passed and the water mostly receded, he dug in the wash bed, a few scoops, and there it was, cool water filtered by the grains of sand.

His clothes had not dried entirely by dark. It was cool and damp out, and he had awakened shivering in the night, feeling the world outside clashing with him, draining that reserve of energy he kept hidden deep inside.

On the second day, he came to the mountain—a great black wedge pushing up from the ground. From the northwest it looked wider at the top than at the middle—imagine, an entire mountain balanced like a canyon-country rock—a huge wide stone on a thin pedestal. And so the O'Odham called it "Baboquivari," which described it in their language.

For the O'odham, the People of the Earth, this was the center of the universe. It was in a cave, hidden but known, high on the steep mountain slope, that I'itoi settled to live the rest of his life underground after giving life to first man.

Bowman had climbed the rough, rocky hillside, sweating under the summer sun. A friend of Bowman's, Ryder Joaquin, had brought him here the first time. He'd met Ryder while wandering the reservation with a botanist named Grey Napoleon, working on a story about how water was quickly disappearing beneath the desert's parched surface.

The O'Odham, for centuries desert farmers, were being cheated out of their share of the dwindling water supply. Bowman's story had made a difference in a water-rights lawsuit, and so he was considered a friend.

Ryder was short and stocky, with rich brown skin like his ancestors'. He had led the way to the cave, singing an ancient song, his voice echoing off the mountain slopes.

That first time, Bowman only ducked his head into the cave, not wanting to enter too far, feeling a need to show the measure of his respect. It is tradition to leave a gift for I'itoi, and he had pulled the new leather belt from around his waist and left it there in the cave among the offerings of others—a hat, some flowers, rosary beads, and decorative strings that hung from the ceiling.

Having walked across the desert, Bowman wondered what offering he could leave this time.

Finally, he sat on a rock in the afternoon sun and slowly bent down to unlace his shoes—hightop Nikes he wore for hiking. They weren't new, but not really old yet either, still with plenty of tread. He rolled up his socks, wet with sweat and brown with ground-in dirt, and stuffed them in the shoes. Then he pushed the shoes and socks inside the cave and picked his way carefully back down the mountain.

It was the first time he had walked a long distance barefoot. It turned out to have some advantages. No sand in the shoes, no burrs in the socks. He stepped carefully. Instead of crashing through the brush and cactus as usual, he picked his way cautiously, staying on the soft, warm desert sand.

And when he got back, she was still there.

That time had been the worst, and he had come to think of it as the Fight. And they'd remained together since . . . with a different understanding. There were strings, but they didn't tie each other up with them. They kept separate houses and came and went as they pleased. There was a line between them that shifted fluidly and was hard to see. Where did they stand? When did they trust? How much? It was a line neither crossed.

But lately Bowman had begun to feel dependent on Theresa, if only on her being there when he returned home. He had begun to think again about permanence.

Sometimes it was a little shaky. But then, the way Bowman figured it, so was everything else in his life.

And ultimately there was always the great wide desert surrounding him. Where there was space to walk, and walk.

Thirteen

The offices were dark and Bowman fumbled for the light switch. It seemed to move erratically from one wall to another in his absence.

He stumbled over something soft, twisted in the air, arms flailing outward, and landed against a hard, cold surface.

A drawer knob dug into his back and he let out a soft grunt, sliding to the floor at the foot of the desk. His ankles rested on the long, bumpy bag of fertilizer he had tripped over, his feet sinking into it a little. Fertilizer?

He felt something creeping down his neck, over his ratty collar, and nearly jerked around, wanting to switch on the lights and identify the bug or spider before it bit him.

But the notion drifted away, and he realized vaguely that it was blood slinking down his collar from the cut where he had hit his head.

Bowman leaned back, panting. He turned his head gently from side to side, feeling intently for any serious damage. It seemed okay, but when he put his hand to the back of his head, he found a wet spot of matted hair.

He closed his eyes, concentrating. Now he understood.

The light switch was on the left, above the file cabinets. He had been fumbling along the wall to the right, above the watercooler. That's where the light switch was at home— just inside the door to the right. It seemed like he did this every time. With one exception. That left unexplained the sack he had tripped over.

He saw silhouettes of office furniture around him, the city lights filtering in through the tall, shuttered windows of the Weekly Building. *Casa de Weekly. Mi casa,* Bowman thought, then he found that amusing and began to giggle. But that hurt his head, and made his eyes swim in and out of focus. He concentrated on taking deep, slow breaths, and not moving at all.

There was a light. Dim, unfocused. A blur of green-white, flickering again, then going black. If he had to guess, it was in another room. The one next to this was Layup, where the paper was put together on wide flats before it was sent off to the printer. Beyond that, Allen's office. Editor-in-Chief. Editor and Publisher. The light might be from there. Mottled windows between each successive office turned objects on the other side into ghostly dark figures swimming about in an opaque pool.

Breathing. At first he felt with each deep breath a soft wave of pain rushing up through his body to his head. Then the pain receded and there was just the rhythmic throbbing where the bleeding was already beginning to slow. And something else. A pulsing at his ankles, his feet. He tried to think straight. Had he broken something low, twisted an ankle? No. Nothing.

Then he heard the noise and he rolled quickly to his side, pulling his legs toward his chest. Another shriek of pain shot upward and exploded in his head. He lay still, waiting for his mind to clear.

Then he heard it again.

Breathing.

Finally he was able to look down. A door opened somewhere behind him and light spilled into the room. Near his feet was the thing he had tripped over. It was Allen.

The editor's face was bulging and red. His breath came in raspy, labored gasps. What was that around his neck? Something black. A cord, Bowman could see that now, the twisting loops running off to an office phone in pieces on the floor.

The man's—Allen's!—eyes twitched his way, bulging in the dim light, and Bowman began to crawl toward him. Allen? Nonsense. Burglary? Murder? His head swam. He forced himself to move through the pain, knowing only that he had to get to that cord, pull it loose, unwrap it.

Then there was a noise behind him, from back in the light somewhere, and he felt the red shock as his head was struck for the second time that night.

Then nothing.

Fourteen

Some call it Buckthorn cholla, or jumping cactus, Bowman wrote. *It is one more sign that the desert belongs to no man. To the botanist, it is* cylindropuntia Acanthocarpa, *and its skinny, tubular stalks spread like needled intestines across the sand and rock.*

The sharp spines grow more than an inch long. Barbed at the end like fish hooks, they pierce the skin deeply. When they grab you, a little chunk of intestine breaks off the stalk and jumps onto you, into you, and hangs there while its mild poison seeps into your skin.

At the moment, Bowman was getting a close look at a clump of jumping cactus. Too close.

He felt the sharp spines, the tingle of the irritating poison in his chin. Looking down over his nose, he could just make out the single chunk of cholla attached below his mouth. He tried to twist his head, to shake the thing loose, but he was hit by a wave of nausea that swept from his stomach through his spine and high up into his head, where the throbbing continued.

". . . is waking up, see?" The voice penetrated the dense red haze surrounding Bowman's brain.

"Otro," another voice said. *"Uno mas."*

He felt the thick hand dig into his hair, push him forward. The cactus swam into view. He had time to close his eyes and grit his teeth as his face was about to plunge into the spiny plant.

At the last moment, Bowman turned to the side, a monumental effort, catching the blow mostly with ear and jowl. When he was pulled away, he could feel the sagging weight of a second piece of cholla hooked onto his cheek.

"Le gusta? Le gusta?"

He tried to remember what it meant. Even with his broken Spanish, he was able to figure it out; someone was being asked if they liked something. Liked what? What the hell was there to like?

"Otra vez? Otra vez?" Again? he thought. No, not again, and he realized they weren't talking to him and that they didn't really want an answer.

"Uno mas?"

"Si. Uno mas."

Bowman squeezed his eyes tight and waited. The thick hands grabbed him again, lifting him by the scruff like a kitten. Then the forward motion, sensed, though dimly, by the equilibrium, the vital fluid of the inner ear.

This time he felt his entire face shoved into the cholla. It felt like a thousand, a hundred thousand, red-hot stingers penetrating the finely nerved, soft flesh of his face and forehead. He wanted to scream, overtaken by rage and hot, fevered pain. He felt nauseous, tasted bile rising, but he clenched his jaw tightly so that the spines sticking into his lips could not penetrate the tender inside of his mouth.

Then he was pulled away from the cholla, flipped over, and dropped onto his back on the desert ground.

Bowman felt the little cylinders of cactus hanging by their spines, the weight tugging at the skin of his face, lips, forehead.

"Ahorita!" one voice said.

"Now, you see," the other said, "that there are places you should not stick your big fat nose into. You understand?"

Bowman groaned.

"This is personal, okay? This is not a part of the job, but this is just for me. You understand?"

Again Bowman groaned.

"I come all the way up here just to see you. You been asleep a long time. I think maybe you never wake up. But I hope you do. This is personal, you understand?"

He wanted to yell out *Yes, yes, goddamnit. Of course I understand.* Even if he didn't, it was all perfectly clear. *Okay—anything, damn it, but just don't put me in the cactus again!*

He felt pressure on the big chunk of cholla clinging crossways above his eyes, the spines poked down, just touching the lids. He squeezed his eyelids tighter, anticipating the pain, expecting the cactus to grind into his eye sockets.

Instead, there was a tugging, and then relief as the chunk was gently plucked away.

"You understand?" the voice asked. "I just want to make it real clear. This is for me. I want you to know you really don't get away. No one does."

And even as he blinked and opened his eyes, Bowman

recognized the voice and knew where he had seen the face before. It was the suit from the border, the big man with the mustache.

The guy had to be Mexican police, Bowman thought. State? Federal? Most likely state. The Feds didn't get so deeply involved in the corruption anymore; in fact, many of them had been working to end it, and they were more sensitive now to the border and political relations with their northern neighbors. State police could still be bought, though. At bargain prices.

This man was plainclothes, and he must have some powerful friends to have gotten up here so fast. Bowman remembered the thick muscles under the soft-looking belly, and the way the man had thrown him around like a bag of groceries, carrying him back toward the border.

The suit picked Bowman up by his shirtfront, pulled him close. In the periphery of his vision, Bowman could see the little cylinders of cholla still sticking to his cheeks. For a second he thought the man was going to make a mistake, pull him too close and poke himself with cactus. Instead, he held him there, looking Bowman in the eye from just beyond the haze of spines.

"If it's up to me, *esta muerto*. Get it? Dead man. But I just get paid to do a job, so you get to live. But I ever see you again, and maybe I'm not working . . . you ever come to my country again . . . then you're not so lucky. Get it? Or maybe someday I will—how do you say?—take my vacations. Maybe someday I come visit you when I'm not working. We see.

"But I got a message for you, okay? Now we done with the games. My job is this message. I make sure you get this message, make sure you understand, okay? Okay?" The suit reached around behind Bowman, grabbed a handful of thick, long hair at the nape of his neck, and twisted it roughly.

Bowman gasped at the pain, spewing out spittle and snot. "Okay," he rasped. "Okay."

"The message is, you in a lot of trouble now. So maybe it's time for you to leave. Maybe you been sticking your nose into the wrong business. So now maybe you take your vacations. For a long time. Someone will get in touch with you when it's time to come back. If there is a time to come back. Get it?"

Bowman nodded.

"You know," the suit went on, "when I heard it was you, I come here immediately. I say, 'You hold him for me. He wakes up, you hold him for me. Because this is personal. And I gotta show him. Nobody beats me. Not no drunk gringo. Nobody.'

"So now you gotta go, see, and take your vacations. But you know something, Mister Bowman?" He paused. "Don't take your vacations in Mexico."

Then he dropped Bowman to the ground, keeping hold of the hair at the back of his head until the last minute, spinning him over so that he landed on his face with a soft thud.

Bowman grunted and spat in pain.

Then he passed out.

He stumbled out of the desert in an undeveloped area northwest of town. His face was covered with little red welts where he had pulled the pieces of cactus away before passing out the second time.

After regaining consciousness, he had walked east for no other reason than that he felt Tucson should lie in that direction.

He found a road he recognized, and his instinct was confirmed. Then he followed the crumbling blacktop, walking along the rocky dirt shoulder until he came to a convenience store. He washed off his face and arms as well as he could at the spigot outside the store, watching dirt and dried blood drain between his feet, across the sidewalk to the parking lot.

Then he made the phone call.

She'd been worried when he hadn't shown up, and she sounded concerned as he told her about what had happened. But her responses were strange, as if she weren't really listening to what he was saying.

"Nate," she kept asking, "what are you going to do?"

"Well, damn, Theresa, I was hoping for a ride into town. But if I can't get one, I guess I'll call a cab. Maybe just walk. It couldn't hurt."

"That's not what I'm talking about. Nate, do you know how long you've been out there?"

"I don't know, most of one night and a day, maybe two nights? I'm not sure. Jesus, Terry, are you listening to me? I said Allen's dead."

"I know. Have you seen the paper?"

"What paper? It hurts just to talk. I haven't seen anything."

"You haven't seen the *Daily Sun*?"

"No." And then he got that sinking feeling as she told him what he would read there.

"There's something else," Theresa said. "Porter Eisor wants to see you. He's asking me to arrange for you to come in and see him. He says it's about the story, Nate. He says he thinks he can help you."

Fifteen

Bowman leaned back against the leg of the statue. His body was sweating under the midday sun, but he was not conscious of the temperature. The heat was as much a part of him as his hair, hands, feet. Noticing the heat would be like noticing he had fingernails.

In addition to the pain and swelling in his face and his knee, however, the horse's hoof was digging into his lower back, ruining an otherwise perfect resting place.

It was humid, the air thickening as dark rain clouds thundered up from the south, a broad wall of black and gray growing in the distance.

He looked at his watch. Five minutes past three. Almost time. Eisor had wanted him to arrive at a quarter after. He would wait a few more minutes, then cross the large plaza, enter the air-conditioned atmosphere of the skyscraper, and ride the elevator to the top floor.

He could almost pick out the window, thirty floors above, where the fat man would be sitting in his office, perhaps even now looking down on Bowman and the plaza of the Twin Towers, out at the city beyond, and beyond that at the mountains and the mine.

Bowman had arrived early, an old reporter's habit, and now he had some time to kill. He didn't mind. It would give him a chance to pull his thoughts together.

But his mind kept straying to the statue he leaned against, drawn there by the large bronze hoof digging into his kidney.

The statue was huge. A giant of a man on a powerful horse. Francisco Vàsquez de Coronado. Coronado the Conqueror. His battered bronze visage reflected fierce rays of sunlight in the plaza.

Coronado had gambled everything, heading north from New Spain, now called Mexico, into vague, unknown lands looking for a fabled province where the cities overflowed with wealth and the streets were paved in gold.

He had found only the hard, angry desert Bowman called home. But Coronado had continued on, and he explored unknown regions maybe as far north and east as Kansas. Members of his party stumbled upon the Grand Canyon and encountered the People of the Pueblos.

So Coronado had become the conqueror and earned for himself the right to sit here among the towers of steel for a time, a great lance at his side struck to the ground, its sharp tip thrusting skyward like a finger pointing toward God, hinting at destiny.

And Bowman sat as if he were a lowly serf at the foot of Coronado's horse, a position he was content with, waiting for an audience with the new conqueror.

Men like Eisor, Bowman thought, would someday have their statues placed side by side with that of Coronado, their great bellies bursting from vests and jackets, cigars jammed to jowl, looking for all the world like desk-bound Sancho Panzas. The new conquerors.

He checked his watch again. Time.

Porter Eisor, dressed in an expensive-looking blue suit, sat behind a tremendous desk, his back to Bowman, peering intently at a computer monitor.

He's looking at it as though it were a snake, Bowman thought, *coiled and ready to strike.* And to Eisor, he figured, it probably was. Eisor's was a world of numbers, where power was measured in stacks of hundred-dollar bills and wealth came in seemingly unlimited quantities, by the acre.

The fat man hadn't moved when Bowman crossed the threshold, ushered into the room by a pretty blond woman with an icy smile that made Bowman wince. Eisor continued to stare intently at the screen, showing no sign that he was aware of his caller's presence.

Bowman looked around the room. It had the appearance of a carefully constructed set. It was as if a photographer, artistic director in tow, had left just moments before, having just shot the cover of one of the slick mail-order catalogues the country was slowly burying itself under.

Along one wall was a series of autographed photos of sports figures. There were miniature replicas of hundred-thousand-dollar luxury cars. And electronic toys. Crystal, and silver, and gold.

But Bowman noticed an exception to the carefully collected paraphernalia of the garishly rich. The far end of the room was different. That wall, facing the office door, was covered entirely by an immense wooden bookcase.

Books ran from floor to ceiling, their ranks broken only by dark wood shelving every foot and a half. Books, books, and more books. Books of every shape and size filled the shelves. Thick, oversized volumes pressed belly to brow with pamphlets and miniatures in a staggered jumble that was disconcerting to the eye, but, Bowman thought, pleasing to the soul.

To Bowman, books were like the heat, and the walking. They were just part of him, in his nature, in his blood. He remembered lying on the floor as a child while his father and sisters sat watching the new black-and-white television—"top of the line," the old man had said, "top of the line." But to Nate it had been just snaps and pops—fuzzy light and background noise. He'd pressed his nose into a small paperback novel with a picture of Wyatt Earp on the cover, six-guns blazing.

Later, in college, he'd spent long hours in the stacks at the library, researching odd scraps of history that seemed to have slipped away. Then he'd moved to Arizona to start work as a reporter, and when he wasn't working or wandering in the desert, he'd roamed the darkened shelves, the dimly lit corners, of the used bookstores and the perpetual fluorescent daylight of the libraries.

Bowman could see at a glance that these were not the books of the poseur, the snotty, insipid pseudo-intellectual who buys books by title and cover rather than by content. Nor was this wall created, as the rest of the office seemed to be, by an interior decorator looking for an image. These books were too ungainly. Decorators picked out whole cases of volumes bound exactly alike—picked them along with the art to match the wallpaper and the carpeting.

Bowman was drawn to the shelves. He looked over the titles and was quickly lost.

Here was a first American edition of Padre Kino's *Historical Memoir of Pimería Alta,* in beautiful condition—only seventy years old, but worth at least five hundred dollars. And Garces' diary, printed under the title *On the Trail of the Spanish Pioneer,* edited by Elliot Coues; two big blue volumes with gold lettering on their spines. Further examination showed that the pages were unclipped, virgin, four hundred dollars minimum.

There were first editions of Garrard's *Wah-To-Yah* and Lumholtz's *Unknown Mexico.* There were leatherbound, boxed copies of books by J. Frank Dobie and Lawrence Clark Powell. Here was a straight run of the works of Edward Abbey, from *Jonathan Troy* through *The Monkey Wrench Gang* to *Hayduke Lives!* All first editions, all in fine condition.

There were more recent books as well. A beautiful volume with a clunky name and a somehow peaceful purple cover, *Beliefs and Holy Places,* signed by the southwest's great folklorist, Big Jim Griffith. And a clothbound edition of Bernard Fontana's book of the O'odham, *Of Earth and Little Rain.* There were books by Gary Nabhan and Janice Bowers. There was even, surprisingly, a copy of *Rape of the West,* by Sal Hand.

Rape of the West was the result of years of intense study of the damage that ranching was doing to public lands. It was a damning tome on overgrazing, and after its release, just about any rancher in southern Arizona would freely admit that he'd just as soon have Sal Hand for dinner as a steak, given the option.

The great irony was that the ranchers and the preservationists were now, just a few years later, coming together to fight the new true despoilers of the desert, the army of developers marching on the last of the open range.

The big, slick, softbound book was signed by the author and inscribed, "For Porter Eisor, may you rot in hell." Bowman laughed out loud.

It was odd that Eisor, the developer, would buy a copy of Hand's preservationist book, and then have him sign it. But the vast wall of books belied the crudeness, the arrogance, and the thick rhetoric that was Porter Eisor.

These were good books, some of them great books. And here was the jewel. Turned face out and encased in a sealed square of clear plastic with a felt bottom, the book was tattered and without a cover. Its pages were dappled with the brown stains collectors called "foxing."

It was not a book actually, but a report, and as Bowman read its title, a wave of cold excitement passed through him. Typically, he was not impressed by material things. To Bowman, collectors were just bored rich people and broke recluses looking for a way to communicate with a world they didn't understand.

But the true historian, the lover of the past and its wealth of wonders was a different creature altogether. With more money, and more time, Bowman figured he might be such a creature. Might be. And the physically small but historically huge objects that were directly linked to the myths taught as history in every grade school in the country, the kind of relics usually found only in museums, sometimes struck Bowman with a force he didn't understand, as if they possessed a talismanic power, a tingling paranormal residue of their time.

This was one of those talismans. But it had to be a fake. No copy existed. If the little card filled with neatly typed information and placed flat before the document was to be believed, here was the original handwritten copy of the *Relaciòn,* Cabeza de Vaca's report of his journey across the face of the North American continent.

This, however, was not the 1542 version presented to Charles V, and printed for public consumption at Zamora. Nor was this the slightly altered version published thirteen years later. Either of those would have been priceless books, museum pieces. But here was something better. The card said that this was the earlier joint report, probably penned by Castillo, as evidenced by the writing style, and delivered by Cabeza De Vaca at Santo Domingo on his way home.

This was the true first of an impossible volume.

Bowman was shaken by the enormity of those thirty pages of tattered paper. He was standing in the same spot reading the note card for the third time when he heard a soft shuffle behind him, felt the warm breath at his ear.

"Mister Bowman, how kind, how very, very kind," the fat man said. "Welcome to the monkey house."

Sixteen

It was a perfectly smooth, cultured voice. Genteel. Designed, it seemed, to startle at all times with its suddenness. Bowman resisted the urge to jump away, turning instead to ask a question.

"There aren't supposed to be any of those . . ."

"In existence?" Eisor said. "No, I suppose not. Not many individuals know about that as yet. A very dear friend discovered it for me. I purchased it recently, with the funds from the sale of a small parcel of real estate. I don't think the seller knew its value. But then, that's the secret to getting rich—knowing the value of things.

"Sit, sit!" the fat man led him across the room to a comfortable seat, then moved behind the desk and dropped into a giant reclining office chair. Now Eisor appeared to be noticing him for the first time, the filthy clothes, the battered face.

"Well, Mister Bowman, you do look the worse for wear."

"Thanks," Bowman said.

Eisor waved the sarcasm away.

"Do you have any idea of why I've asked to see you?"

Bowman shrugged and shook his head.

"No man is an island, Nate. May I call you Nate?"

Again, Bowman shrugged.

"Of course it is because I need your help. Is it so unbelievable that I should admit such a thing?"

Another shrug.

"But I do. I need help, and you, Mister Bowman, can help me."

"No offense," Bowman said, "but I really doubt it. And even if I could help you, I probably wouldn't want to."

"Oh, probably not," Eisor said with a sigh. "But I think you will assist me, Mister Bowman. Because, in exchange, I am in a position to help you." Now the fat man leaned forward. "And, Nate," he said, "you need my help."

"Well," Bowman said, already tiring of the game. "Again no offense. But I really doubt it."

"Then," Eisor said quickly, "if you don't need *my* assistance, why not let your reporter's curiosity take over? Maybe I can tell you something you want to know. Something about things that go bump in the night in places no man should be." He leaned forward again. "Places like the *tinajas*."

Bowman stared at the fat man, waiting.

Eisor smiled, relaxing. "Lately," he said, "the ignorant armies have been clashing by night. That is a problem. It is a problem, Nate, because they have been clashing by *my* window."

"It sounds like you have neighbor trouble. Call the cops."

"Well put. Neighbor trouble. It cuts right to the heart of the matter. But it is a telltale heart, Mister Bowman, and it keeps beating, beating. What I need is to have this heart excoriated. The time for treatment has passed. We must amputate."

"Look, I'm not a cop, and I'm not a surgeon, and I don't have time to—"

"First," Eisor said, his voice rising sharply, "as a sign of good faith, I will supply the aforementioned aid. I'm afraid it will be a bit of a riddle to you, as it is to me, but I know this much—certain acquaintances of mine work for a certain government agency along the border. They have related to me information they acquired from friends of theirs in similar jobs with our neighboring government.

"Their information pertains to the discovery of a recently deceased individual. The remains of this man were found near the *tinajas* of the Pinacate Mountains."

Bowman leaned a little closer. Eisor saw his attention growing, and he smiled.

"They also said there was a second individual involved, and that an attempt had been made to detain this person at the border. A rather poorly handled attempt that raised the ire of a number of officials on both sides of the border.

"While reading this morning's newspaper, I saw this article." Eisor pulled a newspaper from the desktop and tossed it to the floor in front of Bowman. "And I put the two together."

Bowman wasn't surprised; he had seen the newspaper in the rack outside the convenience store and had peered through the scratched plastic at the headline: Local Man Sought in Killing of Editor; Possibly Connected to Border Shooting.

It didn't sound good. The story was short, all of it on page one—The editor had been found dead in the office, Bowman, last seen entering the building after a hotly disputed City Council meeting, was wanted for questioning in the case. And there was his picture in black and white—looking different, though, the face not swollen and scabbed with cactus welts.

He'd noticed one other thing about the story. It didn't have a byline.

"You know of me, Mister Bowman?"

Bowman nodded.

"Know of my connections, my resources?"

Again the nod.

"Then pay close attention to what I say. You cannot trust anyone, Nate—least of all me, I suppose—but in this, I am candid. The police and your old friends—none of them are certain to be outside the loop, none can help you.

"The article is not a surprise to you, I can see that. So you have read it already, probably several times. And you have probably noticed many strange things about it, not the least of which is its lack of a byline."

Bowman's eyes widened a little at that. Again Eisor smiled.

"Oh, yes, I notice many things," the fat man said. "The story is also too short. It carries no details. It is lacking in attribution, its sources only partially disclosed. It is calculated to make you look desperate and dangerous without actually saying so.

"And of course the editors ran from it, as from a hot poker, not wanting to be branded. It is anonymous because they do not know how this will turn out. None of us do. But we all have to see each other at the same parties, those of us who remain, and it could be so embarrassing. And at the risk of repeating myself, you will have to carry this through on your own; you must trust no one."

"Frankly, I don't have any idea of what I'm supposed to carry through," Bowman said.

"Unfortunately, I can't tell you too much," the fat man replied. "I'm afraid my acquaintances haven't been inclined to provide me with more details. I can, however, tell you this much. The entire commotion is actually over land rights."

Bowman stared at the fat man. Apparently this was supposed to mean something to him.

"It's an interesting speech," Bowman said. "But to tell you the truth, I really don't know what you're talking about."

"*Ejidos,* Mister Bowman. I am talking about *ejidos.*"

Seventeen

Bowman left the crisp, artificial atmosphere of the great glass tomb.

Squinting at the darkening sun, he felt humid air wrap around him like a warm, damp blanket.

The monsoons. He could smell the creosote, the desert. It smelled like rain. The wind came in gusts, blasting through the courtyard, carrying dust and dirt and lunchtime refuse—empty paper cups and wrappers, crumpled bags—a giant whisk broom sweeping the city clean for the coming rain. Then a moment of stillness, and another blast, tugging at the clothing of the minions of the great glass buildings as they passed from one air-conditioned structure to another.

His back to the wind, Bowman walked across the court-yard, mulling over what Eisor had said. *Ejidos.* Bowman didn't know much about them. They were deeds to property, dating back two hundred years or more, to the time when the area now known as the southwestern United States was under Spanish rule.

There had been a big commotion over them in New Mexico not long ago. All the conflict that John Nichols wrote about in the *Milagro Beanfield War*. That was it. Not much to go on. Not enough to figure out what Eisor was getting at.

And why had he been so cryptic?

Bowman wasn't sure what old land grants could have to do with it all. But he knew where he could find out.

His thoughts were interrupted by a sound like a *pop* somewhere far off and up, then a shattering noise floating down after it. He looked back in time to see the shards of a mirrored window floating gently in the air, swimming in an almost fluid pattern, twisting in the overcast sky so that they winked like water splashing from a dark stream. Then they were ripped apart by a blast of wind.

Falling more freely was the great dark shadow. It plummeted toward the courtyard like a huge blue bag of cement, neither twisting nor resisting, but coming straight down like an advertisement for gravity.

Bowman watched the fat man fall, noiseless, without protest, toward the plaza.

Right at the end it seemed that Eisor's hand might have twitched—as if now, with his fate certain, he was making one last, hugely understated attempt to simply reject it. Trying to clear away his death as he would a disorganized desktop. But it might have been Bowman's imagination. Probably, he thought Eisor didn't know, didn't see.

Likely Eisor was already dead and wasn't aware of the statue rushing up at him, did not feel Coronado's lance, centered to strike, as it drove into his great stomach, spearing him. And likely the fat man did not suffer the indignity of knowing that after shattering Coronado's arm, he came to rest on the ground with that huge bronze spear rising through him, still pointing skyward, still hinting at destiny.

Then there was the smacking noise and the shock of the impact, which seemed faint and far away to Bowman, who stared in disbelief at the scene before him.

The crowd gathered quickly, like fraternity brothers jostling for a better position around a beer keg. Bowman walked over slowly.

The gawkers stopped in an eerily perfect ring about ten feet away from Eisor, outside the immediate carnage but close enough for a good look. One or two edged nearer, as if instinctively wanting to help. Then—forget it—went no farther. Bowman pushed through to the front of the wall of people and stopped.

So much, he thought, for knowing the value of things. And so much for the embarrassing cocktail parties Eisor had mentioned.

As sirens rose in the distance, he broke free, backing away from the grisly tableau. The courtyard was filled with gawkers, office drones elbowing each other for a better view of the greatest lunch-time attraction of their lives, an untoppable coffee-break story.

A few were starting to cry, and others comforted them, but most, like Bowman, were paralyzed by shock.

Then something—a voice—broke through the haze, cut into the sense of complete and utter unreality that had engulfed Bowman. He heard it again, still faint, but closer now.

He looked up.

Across the courtyard, in the direction of the voice, were two men. They ignored the body. They were dressed in slightly worn suits, one blue, the other gray. Both had on dark ties and sunglasses, and they were walking quickly from the Tower, eyes locked on Bowman.

"Mister Bowman. Bowman!" the one in gray, the taller of the two, called out. He had short blond hair, balding at the top with a pink sunburn that was showing through. The second one was shorter, with darker hair and a slight limp.

Bowman didn't know these men, didn't know how they knew his name. And with a quick chill, he had a feeling that he didn't want to meet them. Perhaps, since they were coming from the direction of the Tower, they had recently introduced themselves to Porter Eisor.

Suddenly, standing amid the crowd, traffic grinding by in the street, the hustle of downtown all around him, Bowman felt very alone. And very frightened.

He looked back one last time at Eisor's body. Even if the two men were just cops, he knew he had to get away from them. Things were spinning out of control, and he felt as he had at the border. If he gave in, he would simply be sucked into the system. Then crushed. And forgotten.

His eyes darted around, looking for a place to go, for an escape. A place far away from the two men in the suits who were closing in on him rapidly.

They were watching for it, and they understood. They knew what he was about to do, and they started moving faster.

Then Bowman saw his chance. As the wind picked up and the first few drops of rain splattered the ground, he cut across the street, taking advantage of a small gap in the traffic, and broke into a shambling run.

Bowman limped up the sidewalk, dodging pedestrians.

He bumped roughly into a woman in shorts and a T-shirt, muttered an apology, and stumbled on.

"You're an asshole," the girl said, turning away, and the voice penetrated Bowman's mind, the phrase repeating to the uneven rhythm of his feet as he ran. *You're—an—ass—hole,* again and again, a mantra by which to time his stride. Then the voice shifted an octave, into a shriek, and it was the voice of his second wife as she had walked out the door. *You're an asshole,* and now he was moving a little faster, voices twisting in and out of his mind as if in fevered dementia. *Good-bye, Bowman*—Theresa—*It's about the story . . . he thinks he can help you. And, Nate*—Eisor—*you need my help.*

As the confusion of voices went on to the rhythm of Bowman's sluggish gait, the wind picked up a final notch, thunder cracked, and the rain came down in a fury. He heard a squeal behind him as the suits knocked down the woman, not pausing to comment, plowing forward after their prey.

Others were running for cover now, ducking out of the rain into buildings.

He was at Broadway, four wide lanes split down the middle by a median of dirt and cactus.

He cut across traffic, onto the median, crashed through the Spanish bayonet growing there, then dodged cars to the opposite sidewalk. He looked back and saw that the men were moving through the snaggle of honking cars behind him. They were nearly to the median. They were close. Too close.

The tall man was reaching back under his coat, pulling a chunk of black metal from the leather holster at his waist.

The rain was coming hard, falling in great sheets, the wind blowing in furious gusts. The cars had their wipers slapping full speed, but even so, it would be difficult to see out of those windshields.

Bowman was suddenly sure he was going to be gunned down in the street. The downpour made a perfect cover. Any driver who could see him would not be able to see the suits halfway across the wide street. And anyone who could see the suit with the gun wouldn't be able to see what he was shooting at.

As the balding suit raised the weapon in the air, Bowman realized the man was thinking the same thing.

Bowman dropped to the ground. He heard the gunshot. Sharp needles jabbed at his head—chips of concrete, he realized, from where the bullet had hit next to him. He rolled backward, away from the street, clunking his head on the post of the metal guardrail.

Then he was falling.

Eighteen

The city itself sits on a floodplain.

The Catalina and Rincon Mountain ranges jut in a rough half-circle around the broad valley.

When the high-pressure systems to the north suddenly disappear in late July and early August, southerly winds push masses of warm moisture up from what was once called the Sea of Cortez.

Now it is the Gulf of California, the long, wide bay stretching northward between Baja California and Mexico's western coast, and it feeds water into the atmosphere. The system rushes north, and rumbling gray clouds reach the city late in the warm summer afternoons. At the mountains, the clouds pause, building, massing, searching frantically for some escape. Then they explode in a torrent of rain.

These are the monsoons, and the name actually refers to the terrifying winds, not to the sacred waters they bring with them.

The city is on a floodplain, and when the rains come they pour down the mountains, the hills, the sloping valleys, through the sandy arroyos, across the city, seeking the low ground.

Many years ago, the town elders in their wisdom decided that the rains must be dealt with, or the city would be submerged. And so a number of Depression-era laborers, courtesy of the WPA program, built a system of tunnels running east-west and north-south beneath the desert pueblo.

The tunnels are large at their openings, where they empty into the washes, large enough for a man to stand up inside. They grow progressively smaller as they wind back up the plain. Near their origins, they are so small that a child could not squeeze through them.

The rain water, in full torrent, rushes through arroyo and gutter to drainage tunnel and on to the big washes, finally emptying into the huge, sand-bottomed riverbed.

Bowman, on his knees in the fast-moving water, looked up at the railing above. He had dropped a good ten feet, rolling in the air like a cat, landing on hands and feet in the wash. His leg throbbed terribly from knee to thigh.

He looked ahead to two openings directly in front of him that were spewing water. No way of telling where they led. Away.

That was good enough for Bowman. He picked the right-hand entrance and rushed headlong into the darkness of the drainage tunnel. The water was at his ankles and rising quickly. He splashed ahead in a graceless run that wanted to be a sprint but was barely a trot.

Soon he came to a connecting tunnel and had to choose again. As he ducked off to the right, he saw the two men in his peripheral vision as they dropped down into the water.

The connecting tunnel ran straight, and after fighting through the water for a couple of hundred yards, in almost total darkness now, Bowman stopped. Behind him he could hear splashing footsteps over the sound of running water, and by bending to just the right angle, he could make out a figure in the dim distance.

They were coming, then. Now he had to think. He'd hoped they wouldn't follow. He'd hoped they would simply wait at the entrance and finally give up. He had imagined that if he holed up long enough (How long? A day? Two? It wouldn't matter, he could do it) they would simply go away.

But they weren't going away. They were coming after him in this dark and hidden place, a perfect place for killing, and there was nowhere to go but further on.

He stumbled on, slogging his wet jeans forward, lifting each foot with an effort against the running water. As he moved, he kept his arms in front of him in the darkness, following the contours of the tunnel by feel.

His hands bumped hard against solid concrete. He followed the rough surface down and found it was about two feet wide. Then there was another opening. This, then, was one of the sections where the tunnel shrank to a smaller size.

With a feeling that would have been paranoid if it weren't rational, Bowman ducked his head and started up the smaller tunnel.

The water was rising, and the panicked feeling of claustrophobia started to grip his throat, a strong, choking hand under his chin.

Again he bumped his fingers against cement, and again the tunnel shrank. Now he was hunched over, and the water was up to his waist. Another foot and it would be up to his neck, two feet and the tunnel would be full.

It must be a truly incredible storm, he thought distractedly. Thoughts slipped in and out of his mind and he realized that he had fallen into the surreal, shocked state where the brain begins to relieve pressure on itself, unguided.

He paused, breathing deeply. Behind him, a little closer now, he could hear the splash of the pursuers.

He pushed ahead, concentrating on moving his legs as efficiently as possible.

For a moment it seemed that he saw some vague light up ahead, a place where the tunnel wall turned from black to gray and then disappeared around a bend. He told himself that it was not really there and put his head down, stumbling on.

It did grow brighter, though; he could see that now. The water was up to his chin and splashing his mouth and nose. It rose more quickly here in the smaller tunnel and was harder to move against.

He broke around the bend to a place where the tunnel opened onto a square the size of a small prison cell.

The dim light shone through the square grating above— he was in a large drainage where water poured down from the streets. The room was half full and rising, and water cascaded in from above and from the tunnel on the opposite side. The current was strong, and he had to fight his way into the opening and then struggle not to be pulled back down.

He looked up, reached. The grating was not high, maybe a foot above the tips of his outstretched fingers. If he could make the jump and keep his face clear of the water pouring down, clear enough to breathe anyway, he might be able to ride the storm out. For a little while. But if he tried and failed, he knew the current would draw him back into the tunnel.

He crouched, feeling a burst of pain in his knee, and jumped.

His fingers slid easily through the wide grating and he clutched hard to one thin bar.

Now the tunnel was nearly full.

He listened, but the splashing behind him was no longer there.

Nineteen

Theodore L. Fountain was a man of earth and letters. Those who knew the historian well called him "Toppy," a nickname he had acquired as a child, when he consistently achieved the highest score in class in every subject. There was, in fact, a four-year run from the sixth to the ninth grade when Toppy did not miss an answer on a single test.

A computer engineer who built missiles by trade, he was a historian by a vocation. He had written a number of small, privately published books on the Pimería Alta over the years, and though his work had never been accepted by the academic historians ensconced in the brick walls of the university, he was a leading, if greatly ignored, authority on the region—particularly when it came to the anthropology of the Sonoran tribes, a subject at which he was unparalleled.

Toppy lived in a sprawling adobe house outside Tucson, a few hundred feet from the reservation. The ranch-style home, which rested quietly among the sage and saguaros, had been built by a pioneer in the Arizona Territory when Apaches still raided unprotected settlements, swarming down like dust devils, then disappearing as abruptly as the wind. Bands of renegade horsemen roamed the Sonoran wilderness then, robbing, killing, and scalping, and Glanton and his mercenaries were still a recent memory.

The man who built Fountain's house had those things in mind when he designed the twisting catacombs of its interior. A maze of walls spread throughout the massive structure, with hallways that went no place and doors that seemed to spring up from nowhere and lead to rooms you expected to find on the other side of the house. There were also several hidden passages, one leading to a room behind the fireplace large enough for an entire family to hide in it. And there was evidence that at one time an escape tunnel had run under the back wall.

Fountain had lived in the house for forty years. He was a brilliant man, but had no sense of direction, and consequently he still didn't know his way around the place with absolute certainty.

Now the historian's lively voice echoed from behind the big wooden front door. "Coming! Don't leave, I'm coming."

Bowman waited patiently. Fountain was somewhere back in the maze of hallways and rooms and would have to make his way out.

The door was massive, made of thick, dark, weathered wood. In the center, at eye level, there was a small lookout hatch, crossed by iron bars.

"Coming!" The voice was closer now, and Bowman smiled.

"Who is it?" The port was filled suddenly with Fountain's expectant face—bald head, wire-rimmed glasses, and bright eyes.

"Bowman!" he said, answering his own question. "Nate,

how are you? Come in, come in!" And he was already opening the door.

From past visits Bowman knew that it would be difficult to get a word in for these first few minutes. So he followed Fountain into the house quietly.

Bowman had first met the historian while working on a story about a vanload of tourists murdered along the Gulf of California. Eight elderly men and women, most of them Easterners with winter homes in Arizona—"snowbirds," as the locals called them—had been found tortured to death. The killers had used straps of leather from luggage and camera cases to tie them up, hanging them by their hands to fence-post-sized stakes planted in the ground and slowly carving them up with hunting knives.

The problem was, there wasn't much more than hands left of them.

Rumor had quickly spread that it was the work of the Seri Indians, a once savage and reclusive tribe that had inhabited *Isla Tiburon,* Shark Island, near the gulf's eastern shore. With Fountain's help, Bowman had shifted the blame from the Seris—now peaceful craftsmen living off of the tourist trade in Bahia Kino—to the band of small-time thieves that had committed the crime to cover up a robbery.

Bowman had liked Fountain immediately, liked the way he lived—near the desert and its people—liked it that Fountain always had some new arcane, and sometimes useful, bit of information to share, and they had become friends.

"Hi, Toppy."

"Come in, come in. It's good to see you! What?" He paused, his bright face suddenly concerned. "D-d-did you say something?"

Bowman shook his head softly and smiled to himself. It

was quite possible, he thought, that the historian had a neurological syndrome that made it impossible for him to speak and hear at the same time. Most of the time, fortunately, just listening to the chipper man was good enough.

Fountain's voice was soft and scratchy like wool, and when he threw his head back and laughed, which was often, it sounded like he was gargling cotton balls. He was laughing now.

"Why, Nate," he said enthusiastically, "you look like hell!"

"Thanks."

"So, tell me, how was the *Camino?*" The historian led Bowman back into the maze of hallways as he spoke. After a couple of unsuccessful attempts, he found the small living room.

"How was Mexico, Nate?" He looked closely at Bowman. "Good Lord, there's something's happened. Tell me about it."

And so, sitting in a broad-backed leather chair, nestled safely within the maze of adobe walls, Bowman told the cherubic man his story. Starting from the beginning, from the *Camino del Diablo.*

After telling Fountain about the *tinajas,* and the mules and Vyking, he paused, falling into silence.

The historian rose from his chair, shaking his head sadly, gently. "John," he said softly. "Poor John."

Bowman just nodded. Both men were quiet for a while. Finally Fountain spoke again. "Do you need a drink, Nate?" he asked. "Beer? Water?"

"Water," Bowman said. "Ice, if you have it."

The historian nodded and left the room. He was gone for a while—longer than it should have taken to get the drinks—and Bowman imagined him stumbling through the huge maze of the house, trying to find his way first to the kitchen, then back to the living room.

Fountain returned carrying two tall, handblown glasses, clear but for the little air bubbles and the blue rims at the top. Bowman drank heavily, then sat back.

Then he told the historian about pulling his backpack from under the tree and stumbling through the desert for most of the night, heading west by the stars. He told of how he had watched the backtrail, but no one followed, and of how he fell asleep by a wash a few hours after sunrise, waking late the next day to the thick, damp smell of creosote, the cracking of thunder, and the rain.

"I ended up on the highway to Gringo Pass."

"Not much of a road last time I was on it," the historian said.

"It's not on the tourist run, so it's not getting any better," Bowman told him. "Anyway, a truckful of *campesinos* picked me up, took me to the line. When I crossed, some Sonoran cops tried to stop me. Almost did. Even fired off a round. Almost started a shoot-out with two customs agents. You must have seen it in the newspapers the last couple of days."

"Perhaps," Fountain said vaguely. "I haven't been out."

Toppy didn't have a television, and it never surprised Bowman that news reached him with a stately slowness.

He told the historian about the editor and Eisor, and about the men who had hunted him in the rain, about the single bullet barely missing his head.

Finally he explained how he had escaped into the tunnel, the drain filling quickly with water from the ravaging monsoon. How he had hung from the grating for what seemed a long time—how long? Twenty minutes? Thirty? He couldn't say for sure. As long as it took, anyway. He'd hung on until the storm, short and furious, passed. Then he'd dropped down into the water and trudged on into the shrinking cement cavern, not wanting to go back to the entrance, toward his pursuers, not wanting to face what he might find there.

As Toppy listened carefully, leaning forward slightly in his comfortable chair, Bowman told him of how he had found a steel ladder bolted into the concrete, the ladder leading up fifteen or twenty feet to a manhole cover he had shouldered out of the way with great effort. Bowman told the gentle man how he had wandered down a wet and wind-ravaged street, tree limbs and palm fronds lying at haphazard angles where the storm had quit them, about the tin roof of a warehouse, twisted and chewed into sections, resting against a sagging fence, the skeleton structure beyond staring stupidly at the clearing sky.

As night fell, he'd made his way downtown, sticking to the backstreets, recovering his vehicle and driving through roads wet and laden with brittle refuse, rigid pieces of debris that had not bent before the storm's terrible power and so had been carried onto the streets and walkways of the pueblo.

He'd driven past Theresa's house, seen the lights all out, her car absent, and then travelled on to this rambling maze of adobe by the reservation.

"So now," Bowman said, "my problem is, I don't know what Eisor was talking about. I don't know the first thing about *ejidos*, much less about how they could relate to this mess."

Toppy was quiet for a long time after Bowman was finished. Finally he rose and walked across the room. On the wall above the fireplace hung a glass case with a revolver inside.

"Have I ever told you about this pistol?" he asked. Bowman shook his head, no.

"It belonged to John Ringo. You remember, the man Jack Burrows called 'the gunfighter who never was.' "

Bowman nodded.

"Ringo lived in Tombstone back in the Earp days," the historian said. "He was a young man—just thirty-two years old—when he got up one day, put on a white cowboy hat, and walked his horse to an old cottonwood tree by a stream. He put this gun to his head and pulled the trigger. He was depressed, Nate, he was depressed."

They were both silent. At last Fountain returned to his chair, where he sat back, shifted sideways, hooked one leg onto the knee of the other, and sighed. When he spoke again it was in a quiet, concentrated voice, a voice preparing to relate all that a brilliant mind could recall of a vital subject.

"It's not *ejidos* you're after," Toppy said. "Not exactly. It can't be. Let me explain, and perhaps you'll understand why Eisor used the word. The word itself is important, you see, because it has more than one meaning."

Bowman sat back in his chair and listened.

"Spain, you know, had only just become a single country when Columbus set sail five hundred years ago. When Ferdinand and Isabella married, Aragon and Castile united. It's important, very important, to remember that only one of those houses paid for Columbus' journey. Isabella dipped into the Castilian coffers and funded the voyage herself.

"So when Columbus stumbled onto a whole new world, rather than a western route to the Orient, the province became subject to Castilian law instead of the joint laws of Spain. It was, of course, quite some time before the Spaniards, having sacked central Mexico, started wandering northward. But almost from the start, there were colonists. And the rules of Castile applied to settlement of the lands.

"Usually, a settler would petition the governor for a certain piece of land. After the plot of land had been defined—it runs from this rock to that large tree, and so forth—the governor would check to see that the grant was not already occupied. Of course the rights of Indians to any land were routinely ignored."

He paused and looked up. Bowman nodded.

"Ejidos," Fountain said, "were different from the land grants themselves. *Ejidos* were communal property. Places where horses and cows could be grazed, water drawn for irrigation, and garbage dumped. The word has two meanings in the sense that it comes from the Latin *exitus,* the 'outside.'"

"What about now?" Bowman asked. "Hasn't there been a controversy over *ejidos* in the last few years?"

"Several," the historian said. "Mainly in New Mexico, and some earlier disputes in California. The problem has been one of encroachment upon these properties by developers. The *ejidos,* you understand, are sort of loosely owned by those who use them. Transfer of that ownership, though never strictly defined, has traditionally been limited.

"The problem is, you see, when the United States signed on to the Treaty of Guadalupe Hidalgo and subsequently made the Gadsden Purchase, it annexed a huge, ill-defined, poorly mapped chunk of real estate. And all of the people with legitimate claims in that region—the region we call the

Southwest—were promised they would be able to keep their lands.

"So what happens to the community property? Well, the lands known as *tierras baldías* were definitely public lands in the sense of the government owning them, like national parks or BLM areas. But the *ejidos* were the property of small groups, local communities. As ever, when push came to shove, the judges usually sided with the one who shared a membership at their country club. That was almost always the developer."

"But what the hell can it have to do with what happened out at the *tinajas*?" Bowman asked.

"I'm not sure," Fountain said. "You know I've done the greater part of my research on the O'Odham and the other tribes of Sonora. Land grants just aren't my cup of *chegai*. If there is a local connection, though, there's one man who would certainly know about it."

Bowman raised his eyebrows.

"Burton," the historian said.

Bowman nodded. "I guess I didn't want to drag him into this if I could avoid it. It'll upset him to hear about John."

Fountain nodded. "In a way, they were a lot alike," he said. "John always reminded me of a young Julian Burton."

Bowman nodded quietly.

He left the historian in the living room and found his own unerring way back to the front door. Letting himself out, he paused in the yard to look up at the night sky. It was clear, so clear it looked like the rain had washed every impurity from the sky. Out here by the reservation, you could see the Milky Way. The silver moon ascended in the east.

Bowman climbed into the Land Cruiser, started it with a blast of fumes, and drove away.

Twenty

The thought of home, a small stuccoed bungalow with swamp cooling and a stiff futon for a mattress, was almost irresistible. Almost.

As he pulled off the freeway and into the city lights, Bowman realized that he could not go there. If the police were looking for him, that's where they would start. And that wasn't the worst possibility. The men who had followed him might be there. Waiting.

Instead, he drove downtown, to the arts district, where a big, shaggy guy like himself could disappear. Instant camouflage. He parked by an old warehouse along the railroad tracks.

The massive wooden freight door was up and he could see the artist in the middle of the studio, running a board across a joiner.

"Durand," Bowman said as he stepped into the swamp-cooled openness of the converted warehouse. The artist did not look up.

Sandy Durand's blond hair hung long and straight, held away from his forehead and face by a round cap. Small, wire-rimmed glasses perched on the nose before piercing black eyes. His expression was clipped and concentrated, a hawk homing mercilessly in on its prey.

"I need a place to sleep," Bowman said.

The artist nodded slightly, finished with the board, examined it, and carefully put it aside. Then he looked up at Bowman with a somewhat startled expression, as if surprised to find him standing there.

"Bed's all made up in the living quarters," he said with faint sarcasm, as if giving obvious instructions to an idiot. "Towels and clothes in the bathroom if you need a shower and a change. Food in the kitchen."

"Thanks," Bowman said, grinning.

Durand turned back to his work silently, then looked up again as Bowman reached the doorway.

"You know," the artist said in that selfsame quiet voice, "you really look like shit. You should try to get some rest."

Twenty-One

The house is old adobe, Bowman wrote. *Ancient wiring feeds a flickering bulb above a small wooden desk. You are transported through time. The archaeologist hunches over a stack of papers, "keeping up." A little old man. But when he stands, unfolding to his full height, he is many inches over six feet. Broad-shouldered and spare, his arms are thick rope, his chest a lean tree trunk. The body of an old cowboy.*

Through the screen door Bowman could see the archaeologist sitting at his desk in the dusty light. His white hair, cropped short as always, jutted out at odd angles. Except for the color, it was the hair of a schoolboy. At odds with the hair were the small round glasses balanced on the strong nose, the spectacles of a professor. Contradiction. But then, so much of the old man's life was just that. And in contradiction, Bowman thought, lies truth.

Burton was among the last of a nearly extinct species. A purebred desert rat, he had lived his life exactly as he wanted.

Without worrying about being consistent or pleasing the critics, he had simply done it his way. Bowman had always thought of the photographer as the likely successor to men like Burton. But the photographer was dead, and even that small chance at continuity had died with him.

A world-class archaeologist, the son of a Harvard professor, Burton had dropped out of college in his sophomore year and never gone back. It was not that academics were too challenging. Just the opposite. He'd found the university a stiff, unyielding place, where knowledge and information turned brittle with age.

He started as an excavator, working the early southwestern digs. He was at Snaketown and Casas Grandes. Over the years, he secured himself a place in the lore of southwestern archaeology.

In his time, Burton used methodology that years later would stun the new breed of academic archaeologists. They were shocked because they thought they had invented the advanced methods of inventory. And here was this old man, working on his own, who had beat them to the punch by about fifty years.

When times got hard, he dug cesspools, trenches, anything to keep himself and his family going, always refusing to join the university, with its religious devotion to old information long dead.

He built his small adobe home by hand and watched as the city grew around him.

And when he had time, he walked in the desert. He'd wandered the great, foreboding volcanic wasteland of the Pinacate for sixty years, and he knew that area as well as any man, living or dead.

For a moment Bowman hesitated at the door, not wanting to disturb the old man, not wanting to bring him into this. But he realized he had no choice, Burton knew more local history than anyone alive.

All paths eventually led to the archaeologist's porch. And all travelers were offered a shot of tequila and a beer. As he left the artist's studio earlier in the day, rested and clean, Bowman had known that to get the information he needed, he would have to see Burton.

He knocked softly on the wooden screen door.

"Come on in, Nate. You've been standing out there long enough," Burton said without looking up from his desk. "You know where the beer is," he added, nodding toward the kitchen hallway.

Bowman shuffled down the carpeted hallway, returning with two beers and a tall bottle of tequila.

"How are you, Julian?" Bowman asked.

"I'm fine, by Christ," the archaeologist said, rising from the wooden chair, eyes bright, offering a strong hand. Bowman put down the mezcal and shook Burton's hand, the rough, hard grip reassuring. Then he handed Burton a beer and filled two shot glasses with the yellow liquor.

"The question is, how are you?" Burton said. "And what is it brings you here's so important you stand at the threshold like a newlywed, wondering if you've come to the right place? By the way, you ought to get the muffler fixed on that old mail truck of yours. I heard you coming a mile away."

That explained one thing, anyway.

"Let's move outside," Burton said. "And you can tell me about it." Then he looked closely at Bowman's face. "What'd you do, go for a swim in some cholla?"

Bowman rubbed the sore bumps on his face and shook his head. "I was dunked."

They sat on old wrought-iron lawn chairs, shaded from the sun by the branches of a huge mesquite tree. Bowman took a long draw off his beer, and as a small lizard flickered back and forth across the adobe wall, he told Burton his story.

When he was done he sat back in the chair and was quiet.

The old man had a soft, faraway look in his eyes. Finally he leaned forward and poured them each another shot. He knocked his down, breathed deeply, then spoke.

"Ejidos, you say."

"Something like it. But I can't figure it out exactly. As far as I know, there weren't any land grants in this part of the Pimería Alta."

Burton's eyes twinkled. "Well you're wrong there, of course."

"Wrong?"

"I'd have expected you'd know, Nathaniel. It's been in the news so much lately."

Bowman shook his head. He didn't know what the old man was talking about.

"Well, not the grant itself," Burton continued, "but the land it covered. All the old coyotes say the northernmost land grant in Sonora was right here in this valley. At the base of the Catalinas. Puma Canyon. Where they're going to build those damned hotels."

Twenty-Two

I'll be damned," Bowman said quietly.

Burton raised his eyebrows, then smiled.

"Nathaniel, when I was a very young man—younger than you by more than a few years—I met an old woman must have been ninety. She looked older, though, old as the desert itself.

"Of course it was an unusual circumstance that brought a young gringo to talk to an *abuela* then. The opportunity just didn't come up. As it happened, it wasn't a very happy circumstance, either.

"We were excavating Lizard Village, and I was really no more than a kid, although nobody could have convinced me of that.

"One of the boys I worked with—Francisco Salazar was his name—he was the *abuela*'s grandson. It was his second dig and my first, and he showed me what to do and how to stay the hell out of the way of the archaeologists.

"My father was in charge of that dig. And I guess Francisco knew it, but he never let on and it never came up. I didn't see the old man much. He was mostly at the university studying the artifacts we pulled from the ground. When he did run into me, he treated me just like the other help. Only maybe a little bit harder—which is the way it was. The way it should be.

"Like I say, Francisco showed me the ropes, and there were a couple of boys younger than me, and I showed them. I guess that made Francisco lead mule to the lead mule, and there wasn't much glory in it, just a whole lot of hard work. Layer by layer, brushing the dust off the buried remains of the Hohokam walls, unearthing an ancient mound inch by inch, in the driest, hottest place I'd ever been.

"Francisco and I and the other boys got on pretty good, and we caroused the bars in town some nights. His family had been here a long time and he knew damn near everyone in town. More than once Francisco kept us all out of jail when we let the mezcal do our thinking for us.

"Then one day Francisco was killed at the site. There was some heavy machinery out there, and the dirt gave way and Francisco was crushed. An accident. They happen, Nathaniel, they happen. I've seen it many times.

"I was the one who went in to town, to an adobe house on the south side where Francisco lived. The old woman, his grandmother—I guess she knew what had happened when I knocked on the wooden door, standing there sweating and dirty and pretty shook up. There weren't many reasons a scared young gringo like me might show up on her stoop.

"She was short and brown with gray hair that had only the slightest traces of black in it. She fetched me a cup of coffee, sweet with lots of milk and sugar, and we sat on small wooden chairs and I told her what had happened.

"She was quiet when I finished, and we sat a while watching the shadows creep slowly up the adobe wall across from us.

"Then she started talking. So quietly that at first I wasn't sure if she was talking to me or to herself, or maybe to no one. But as I listened, I understood.

"Her name was Livia Montiel Salazar, she said, and she had been born in a small house on a great wide ranch along the east bank of the Santa Cruz. Near the north end of the valley, at the foot of the mountains.

"That land was the land of her grandfather, and he'd fought off Apaches and outlaws, and one time he'd protected his family from Glanton's band of scalp-hunters —renegades looking for black-haired scalps to sell to the Mexican government as Apaches—any scalp would do, even that of a Mexican.

"Despite her grandfather's efforts, his land began to shrink around him, and not long after the Gadsden Purchase alienated him in his own country, the lands he had once owned all but disappeared.

"Those lands, the *abuela* said—the area that stretches across the mouth of Puma Canyon—those lands still belonged to her.

"After her grandfather died, her father was run off the last of the ranch lands, and he moved his family in to town. He built his home on the south side.

"We were sitting on the stoop of the house he had built, and although the story she was telling me was very sad, she never once let go a tear, nor betrayed any emotion.

"She said she'd gone out to that old ranch house once— just a melting maze of thick adobe walls by then. She had looked for the old lockbox her father had said was buried out there somewhere and that contained the original land grant, signed by the *alcalde* of the *presidio*.

"Of course she never found it, but that didn't bother her—or if it did, she didn't show it. She said there was a copy of the grant in the archives in Mexico City, and there always would be.

"She raised a thin and trembling arm, the brown-spotted skin hanging from her tough bones, and made a small, fluttering motion with her fingers. That land, she said, would always belong to her family. Always.

"She'd had but one son, and that son had but one son, and now both were dead. Francisco left behind only a young wife and a daughter, and so the family name would go no further.

"This valley, she said, had once been a place that was green and lush, though surrounded by harsh desert. Now the desert was everywhere, and the waters were being killed off.

"The wife's name was Antonia. The university gave her nine-hundred and fifty dollars to compensate her for her loss. The price of a man's life and name then. Of course the wife remarried, I guess, and the daughter grew up and had a child of her own. That's how it works, Nathaniel. That's how it works.

"I never talked to the old woman again, never had a chance to. Saw it in the paper when she died, though, a few years later.

"This country belonged to the Apaches, Nathaniel. The Spaniards and the Mexicans never got much of a foothold here. Farthest north they settled in what we now call Arizona was that ranch in Puma Canyon, a few miles away from the *presidio*.

"Now in New Mexico, they had problems. Oñate settled that land all the way up to the pueblos. Colonized it. And there's been hell to pay ever since."

Twenty-Three

After he left Burton's Bowman drove south and west through the sprawling, urbanized desert. Soon he found himself on Speedway Boulevard, stuck in a knot of traffic. Cars were backed up by construction work—a road-widening project that had been going on for a couple of years.

Bowman tried hard to remember a time when the city had been free from road construction. Failed. The hot, black streets were constantly stretched, twisted and re-created to meet the transportation needs of the always burgeoning populace.

He knew he was getting nearer to the bottom of this thing, but there were still too many unanswered questions. What was the meaning of the connection between the development project in Puma Canyon and the Spanish land grant? It had to be more than coincidence. Had Eisor known more than he'd said? Had he known the difference between an *ejido* and a land grant, and if so, what *ejido* had he been talking about? Had he been killed for it?

Then there was the editor, and John, the death of two friends. *Murders,* he reminded himself. Some bastard killed them. Someone had to pay. Were they connected? *Could they be?* Again, there was too much coincidence, and although Bowman had seen enough of life to know that just about anything could, and did, happen, he had a low threshold of tolerance when it came to believing in coincidence. And what of the Mexican cop?

He thrummed his fingers on the steering wheel, impatient with the traffic.

It all has to go back to the border, to the line, my line, Bowman thought, and suddenly he saw the border as it was, the thinnest of distances between two hard hot places, like the barely extant film of oil separating piston rod and cylinder wall, nearing viscosity breakdown as the engine rages, the tachometer hopping against that place where the gauge changes from black to red.

It had to go back to that night, the night of John's death. What had they seen out there? It had looked like a drug smuggling operation. Could it have been something else?

And where in the hell was Theresa?

He jerked the wheel and pulled out of traffic into a gas station, topped the tank and walked over to a pay phone. He dropped in twenty-five cents and dialed.

While the phone rang at the other end, he watched children playing on the green-grass hill of a city park in the distance. Sweat dripped from his forehead, dampened his face and his thick, long hair. To Bowman, the grass seemed to be in a perpetual state of denial over the weather. Perhaps it was painted green. He turned away.

A woman's voice answered the phone at Eisor and Associates, where things apparently were in chaos.

When he asked, the voice said she would put him right

through to Miss Saldivar. A few moments later, the voice returned and asked who was calling.

"A friend," Bowman said.

The voice disappeared again with a click. Bowman waited, waves of heat splashing up at his legs from the asphalt.

Another click. "Perhaps I can take a message," the voice said.

"Is Theresa in?" Bowman asked.

"I'm not sure I can . . . just a moment," the voice said and—click—disappeared.

This time the silence was replaced by a man's voice. "Miss Saldivar is away from the office. Who's calling?"

Bowman hung up. He tried her at home and hung up on her answering machine as well.

Now he had to make the second call. The harder of the two. The one he had been putting off.

The Weekly. He hadn't checked in since Allen's death— *murder,* he reminded himself again.

He needed to take care of the film cartridge he had hidden at home. He had to get someone from the paper to retrieve it for him.

Bowman held his hand over the mouthpiece to muffle his voice and tried to change the pitch of his vocal cords when a female answered the phone.

That would be Martina, Bowman realized, a young woman just out of journalism school and trying to turn a job as *The Weekly*'s receptionist into a full-time reporting position. Meanwhile, she answered phones and wrote a hiking column. She was tough and bright, Bowman thought, and she just might have what it takes.

Either he successfully disguised his voice or Martina was smart enough not to ask questions. In any case, Bowman was put through to Edwin Malricovich, the paper's assistant editor. Mal had been Allen's right hand, and he would be running things now.

"Bowman, damnit, where have you been?"

"Today?"

"You know what I mean, Nate. If you'd been here, if we'd been able to reach you, the story might have run different. Where are you now?"

"I'm in the wind, Mal. But for what it's worth, I don't think things would have gone the other way. Besides, I didn't have any choice."

"Are you okay, Nate?"

"Tolerable. A little tired, very ugly. The usual."

"We can't talk long," Mal said. "I'm busy."

That wasn't right. No matter how busy he was, he wouldn't say that. Not now. He was trying to tell Bowman something. He must think the phone line wasn't clean.

"Got it," Bowman said.

"Do you know how this thing is going to play out, Nate?"

"I think so. I have a few loose ends to tie together, then it's nailed down."

"How much space?"

"Big."

"Are you going to win?" Mal asked.

"It's booking about fifty-fifty right now. But if I can pull it together, get it in the box, we'll be looking at a Pulitzer."

"Okay, Nate. Listen, I have to call the cops. Soon as I hang up. You understand?"

"Yeah. Okay. I'm only wanted for questioning anyway, if the dailies are telling the truth."

"A big if."

"Sure, but that's our job, not theirs."

"Nate, be careful. You've never been this deep in the shit before. Neither have I. We're all pretty shaken up about Allen."

"Me too, friend, me too."

"And Nate . . ."

"Yeah?"

"When you write this thing, don't mix your metaphors. I've got enough to do around here already."

Bowman hung up and drove quickly from the gas station down a side street—just in case the call *had* been traced and the cops were moving in. He would have to find another way to get the film. But first, he had to go downtown.

Twenty-Four

A couple of years before, Bowman had written a series of articles about a Phoenix financier who was amassing a huge and powerful business through land development and loans. The man's name was Charles Keating, Jr.

Bowman had been amazed by the man's charisma and troubled by his shady deals. In one article, he'd called Keating a modern version of the great western con artist. A snake-oil salesman with a pedigree. Bowman had predicted that one day Keating would end up in jail, and that the house of cards the financier had built and called Lincoln Savings and Loan would tumble in a loud and ugly scandal. As it turned out, that's exactly what happened.

While working on the series, Bowman interviewed a number of Arizona businessmen with ties to Keating. He'd tried repeatedly to talk to Dino Diamante.

Records indicated that Diamante had been involved with Keating in a couple of land-swap deal in the late 1980s. But Diamante didn't want to talk about them.

Bowman had kept after him. It was a long series, requiring months of research, and Bowman made it a habit to call

Diamante's office every other day to request, yet again, an interview. He knew that when it came to investigative journalism, persistence paid off. Sometimes.

Then one afternoon he'd received a phone call at his dugout in the Weekly Building. "Andrew Diamante on line one," the receptionist said.

Andrew? Bowman knew that Diamante's son worked in the family organization, but he had never met him.

As it turned out, they had a lot in common. More than Bowman would have expected.

Andrew Diamante had enrolled at Kent State a few years after the shootings. And though he hadn't actively protested the war, over the years he had come to realize, as most people had, that Nam had been a mistake. Mistakes happen.

Diamante had studied journalism and worked on the college paper, then taken a law degree from Georgetown. But he was an Arizona boy, and when he graduated, he had returned home to work for the development empire his father had created.

Like Bowman, Andrew Diamante loved the land and its people. He knew the history of the region, and he and Bowman had talked at length about New Spain and the prehistoric southwest. They shared an interest in the lesser known, but greater adventurers, like Cabeza de Vaca, and Al Sieber. The desert was in Diamante's blood, and he'd returned home from college knowing that it was where he wanted to be.

Still, the Diamantes were the despoilers of the desert, and Bowman couldn't quite let that go. He and Andrew had maintained a nervous sort of friendship, like two soldiers eyeing each other uneasily across the battle line, each surprised and a little unnerved to find someone so much like himself on the other side.

For all that, Bowman sensed in Diamante the one thing he most admired in human beings: integrity.

"I won't lie to you," Andrew Diamante had said in that first interview and instinctively Bowman had known that he wouldn't. "There will be things I cannot talk about, subjects I will not discuss. But I'll tell you which ones they are, and we'll move on. Any question I'm willing to answer, I'll answer honestly."

And he had.

He'd given Bowman a number of leads that panned out on the Keating story, and in a roundabout way, he led Bowman to understand that his father had lost a great deal of money to Keating but was unwilling to enter into the public eye in order to get it back. Diamante hadn't wanted the attention a media-intensive court battle would draw.

Bowman knew now that the events of the last few days had something to do with the proposed development of Puma Canyon. If he could reach Andrew Diamante and talk to him, he might get some help . . . but if Andrew refused to talk to him, that would tell him something, too.

Twenty-Five

Andrew Diamante was tall and lanky, with thick black hair and a drawn face that seemed to convey a mixed message of utter fatigue and total contentment. He wore a black suit, crisp white shirt, and red tie, all of which looked very expensive to Bowman. He might have been an Italian movie star except for the pale complexion and the too-heavy eyebrows.

Diamante stretched back in his tall leather office chair and smiled at Bowman across the desk. "You'll have to give me a dollar, Nate," he said.

Bowman searched his jeans, pulled out a wad of crumpled bills and disentangled a single, handing it to the developer's son.

"As your attorney, I have to advise you to go to the police and turn yourself in. I can arrange counsel for you, to help you through the process."

"Thanks for the advice, Andy," Bowman said. "Can we talk?"

"As attorney and client, or as reporter and prey?"

"Neither. Everything off the record."

Diamante nodded. "What's on your mind?"

"Developing. Puma Canyon. Things that go bump in the night."

Bowman threw the last part out as an afterthought, watching Diamante's eyes carefully for any sign of reaction. He saw none.

"The first two I know something about. I'm not sure what you're getting at with the last."

"Nothing specific, Andy. I'm just fishing. A lot of bad crazy things have happened around me in the last few days. I don't know what's going on myself. I'm trying to find out who does."

"Well, I'll help if I can. And I'll tell you up front if I can't."

"Is Puma Canyon still going to be developed?" Bowman asked.

"We hope so," Diamante said. "But there have been some snags. You know what happened to Eisor?"

"I was there," Bowman said. "I watched him fall from the South Tower. I'd left his office just a few minutes before."

"The *Sun* mentioned that this morning. A tragedy. Apparently the police are interested in talking to you about it."

"I haven't seen the papers, but it doesn't surprise me. Who else is involved in the development?"

Diamante formed his fingertips into a steeple before him, balancing his elbows on the chair arms, pressing index fingers to pursed lips, a man in contemplative prayer.

"I can't say. But if all goes well, it will be a matter of public record in a few days. I can tell you that together with

Eisor, we, my father and I, represented the large majority of financial investment."

Now Bowman thought for a moment.

"The financing is all clean? Good money?"

Diamante smiled at the question. "Money is neither good nor bad, it simply is," he said.

"Money doesn't corrupt people, people corrupt people," Bowman said with irony.

"People corrupt themselves, Nate. And yes, though I'm a little insulted by the question, it's all above board. Clean."

"I'm just trying to get a feel for what might be going on," Bowman said. "Who owns the land?"

"The city holds title. A land swap deal made it available for sale."

"Why would anyone want to kill Eisor?"

"In addition to the obvious reasons? He had plenty of enemies, and a large number of business associates. I don't know if he had any friends."

Bowman looked past Diamante, out the tinted window, at Tucson.

The sun beat bright and hot from the west. The G.W.P. Hunt Savings Building blinked the time: 4:47 P.M., the temperature, 105.

He had to go. He wanted to catch her, and if he didn't hurry, it would be too late. He thanked Diamante and got up to leave.

"Take care of yourself, Nate," the developer's son said. "You really should talk to the police, you know. If you need an attorney, call me, I'll make the arrangements."

"Thanks."

Bowman stopped at the door and turned back with a

final question. "Andy," he said. "What do you know about the *tinajas?*"

Diamante squinted a little, considering. "The only water stop on the worst stretch of the *Camino del Diablo,* right?"

Bowman nodded.

"Hard, rough territory," Diamante said. "Worst stretch of desert along the borderlands." He paused as if considering adding more. Finally he shook his head slowly.

"A dangerous place, Bowman, a dangerous place."

Twenty-Six

She was just walking out of the building when Bowman drove by. He didn't stop. He'd circled the neighborhood twice but had seen nothing alarming.

He reminded himself that he was only being sought for questioning in Allen's murder, and his apprehension probably wasn't at the top of the priority list of the detective assigned to the case. The men who had followed him were nowhere to be seen.

He made a U-turn at the end of the block, waited, then followed her from a distance.

She was dressed in fatigue shorts, hiking boots, and a T-shirt. Her hair was blond and short, and she walked with an arrogant swing in her step. Bowman followed her two blocks east, where she turned into a gravel parking lot, crossing toward a beat-up old jeep. Bowman accelerated and pulled in next to her, then killed the engine.

If Martina was surprised to see him, she didn't show it. She smiled easily.

"Hey, Bowman, how ya doin'? Cops looking for you everywhere, you know."

"I've been told."

"Yeah, well, I'd keep my head down if I were you."

"Thanks. Listen, Martina, I need a favor. It may be a little bit illegal. And dangerous. But it's important. A big story is riding on it."

"Sure," she said. "The more illegal the better." Her grin was cocky.

Bowman explained where the film cartridge was hidden and what to do with it. He warned her that the house was probably being watched and to be careful that she wasn't seen.

"Sure, sure," Martina said eagerly, fumbling in her deep pants pockets for her keys.

"Martina," Bowman said. "Relax . . . and be careful."

He started the Land Cruiser with a rattle of thick smoke and drove away.

Bowman knew that with the photos, he would have a story that would brand a couple of people. Who were they, the two in the background running contraband north from the *tinajas?* Identifying them was the key.

But it would be a better story if he had answers to a few other questions as well. There was one more place to look.

Just in case, he stopped at a hardware store and bought a cheap shovel, throwing it in the back of the Cruiser. Then he wove through traffic across town, heading west, toward the freeway . . . and the road to Puma Canyon.

Twenty-Seven

The headlights pulled up behind him just after he exited the old highway onto the interstate—two piercing bulbs of white growing larger, and finally filling his rearview mirror.

It was a truck or a four-wheel drive of some kind; he could tell by the boxy silhouette. A large vehicle, jacked high with big tires, big enough that the headlights shone straight through the back window of the Land Cruiser. Maybe just kids screwing around, Bowman thought, and even as it entered his mind, he knew he was kidding himself.

His heart hitched and went a notch faster. He eased back on the accelerator.

If it's just another idiot, he'll get bored and pull around. Bowman pushed softly on the brake pedal.

The headlights crept forward, then eased back in response to Bowman's deceleration, holding their position a few feet behind him. *Right on goddamn top of me,* Bowman thought.

Apparently they weren't interested in passing. What then?

He stomped down on the accelerator. The Land Cruiser jerked ahead. There was a great hum as the driver behind him floored it, surging back into position on his tail.

Bowman shot through the great wide curve of the highway along the southwest corner of town, picking up speed as the Land Cruiser slung itself into the straightaway. He could hear the roar of the vehicle behind him, and now, under the street lamps, he could see it in his rearview mirror—a big old V-8 Blazer with jacked-up suspension and the requisite row of KC lights on the roof.

Bowman pulled out of the curve and shot across two lanes of traffic.

The interstate was six lanes wide, three to a side, separated by a thick cement embankment. He raced up the fast lane, gathering speed as the Land Cruiser shimmied underneath him.

The Blazer was stuck two cars back, but it squeezed through an opening, skated into the slow lane, then plunged back across the highway. Suddenly it was next to him.

Under the eerie glow of the freeway lights, the Blazer's dark-tinted windows looked to be a horrible shade of green. The Chevy shifted a little closer and Bowman shot a glance over his right shoulder. Silhouettes were just visible through the darkened glass. It appeared as if the passenger was leaning over to pick something up off the floor. The driver had his face averted, shouting in the other's ear.

Bowman had reached top speed. Seventy miles per hour. Much more and the motor, whining furiously in the night, would snap, piston rings shattering, rods breaking away from shaft, the whole thing seizing, then slowly rolling to a stop.

Bowman checked both side mirrors, looking for an opening in the traffic. Nothing. The next exit was just ahead and coming up fast. But he was trapped by the Blazer on the right and traffic ahead. And now a new pair of headlights had eased in behind him, locking the back door.

He glanced over at the Blazer and saw the passenger handing a flat, black object to the driver.

Frantically, Bowman looked around again. The window of the Blazer slowly slid down. The car behind jumped forward, nearly onto Bowman's bumper, squeezing him.

Bowman had the accelerator to the floor, and the Land Cruiser shook furiously. He checked the speedometer. It had crept up over seventy-five. The engine shrieked.

He glanced to the right and saw the gun.

Bowman stomped on the brakes—a moment after the driver of the car behind him, frustrated and disgusted, jerked over into the middle lane behind the Blazer.

He saw the windshield crack, heard almost simultaneously the slap of the gunshot, felt the reverberation.

Then he was back and fading, the brakes nearly locked, slowing at a dangerous rate.

He stomped on the gas and cut through both lanes, heading for the exit ramp.

Twenty-Eight

The interstate was designed after the great old California freeways. It sits high on a wide dike of concrete that runs in a great arc around the pueblo. On the west side of town it parallels the riverbed. On- and off-ramps climb at sharp angles to join the six lanes of traffic.

Bowman almost didn't make the off-ramp, skittering across the concrete and bouncing over warning bumps. He straightened out, and as he braked hard against the downgrade, he looked in the rearview.

It had been a good cut, damn good, and he didn't think the Blazer would have a chance. He heard a squeal of locked brakes and the sharp crunch of vehicles colliding.

Then the Blazer was at the edge of the freeway, flying over the brink ten or fifteen feet past the exit. It landed with a great jolt, front wheels first, then settled down, the driver fighting hard to keep it from squirreling off the far side of the ramp.

Bowman let up on the brake and looked ahead. The ramp leveled into a hundred-foot straightaway leading to a traffic light. Broadway ran under the freeway here. On the other side of the street, a ramp led back up to the interstate.

He looked at the light. It was red.

Bowman glanced in the mirror again, and the Blazer was on him, very close, the headlights looming in his rear window.

Teeth gritted, shoulders hunched, he slammed the gas pedal to the floor and bolted through the red light.

The intersection was a blur of peripheral colors. He heard nothing—no brakes squealing, no jarring crunch of steel—only the rush of blood pounding in his head, and from farther away the thin whine of the Land Cruiser's motor, the rattling of its doors.

The Land Cruiser climbed the on-ramp, and Bowman watched the Blazer in the rearview. It too ran the red. But the other driver didn't get off as luckily.

Bowman saw the car, a small streak of blue, fly in from one side, clipping the Blazer's rear fender before bouncing away and flipping onto its roof. Sparks fanned orange and bright in the night as the car slid upside down across the street.

The Blazer took the hit hard, slid to one side, then recovered. As the lights straightened out and the vehicle accelerated up the ramp after him, Bowman turned his attention to the interstate, watching for an opening and wondering what he was going to do next.

They wove through traffic at seventy-five.

Bowman cut into the middle lane and the Blazer pulled up on his left. The right lane was empty. The Blazer matched his speed and slowly drifted closer, squeezing him toward the outside.

Ahead, there was another exit, and Bowman drifted into the slow lane and then onto the ramp. The Blazer braked and pulled in behind him, following him off the interstate.

There was no light here, no cross street. The ramp leveled off and the road curved away to the right, following the course of the Ventano Wash.

The wash was small, fifty feet across at its widest. It still flowed with runoff from the monsoon of the day before.

Bowman raced down the single lane, skittered through the curve at sixty-five. The Land Cruiser rattled its protest.

There was another curve ahead, then the road narrowed and crossed the wash on a cement bridge, beyond which were the railroad tracks.

As he pulled through the first curve, Bowman heard the Blazer's engine howl with acceleration.

He fought the curve, pulled into the straightaway, and the Blazer was next to him again, two wheels on the asphalt and two on the shoulder of the narrow road.

Bowman massaged the accelerator. The Land Cruiser shrieked its disapproval. The Blazer, with eight cylinders of hopped-up anger under the hood, kept up easily.

The next curve was coming, and as Bowman turned into it, fighting the steering wheel, the Blazer crashed into his side.

The Land Cruiser took most of the blow on its wide tires.

Now Bowman was half-off the road. He jerked the wheel hard, striking back, but the Blazer was ready for it, and as they careened recklessly through the curve, it fought him off.

The bridge was just ahead. Bowman gave it one more

shot, pulling hard on the wheel, trying to shunt the Blazer aside. He felt the tires slipping beneath him.

Then he was at the bridge, braking hard, pulling to the right, narrowly missing the guardrail and lurching down the embankment into the water.

Twenty-Nine

*The mountain rises from the desert like some dark
god of prophecy,* Bowman wrote. *To the O'Odham,
it is Babat Duag. Frog Mountain. We borrow a
name from the language of the once proud
conquerors—the Santa Catalina Range. And it
beckons like a preordained future.*

Pinpoint light. Bobbing and weaving, shifting, pausing,
hovering. Then receding.

When it returns, it is no longer alone. Two white dots.
Swinging, swinging, loping through the air, growing
larger.

One freezes in the background while the other advances,
growing terribly large now, frightening, like some gigantic,
flexible fireball, white-hot and bounding inexorably forward. For a moment it disappears, then it grows brilliant,
larger than it has ever been, unimaginably large, huge and
fiery and blinding with the force of the sun. Then, with a
tiny, tinny click, it disappears.

"Bowman. Bowman, goddamn you."

He struggled toward the voice. It was a wonderful, reassuring homing signal, a soft and sweet call, a siren, and if he
could only concentrate for a few seconds, he felt sure he
could follow it out of the darkness.

"Wake up, Nate."

Theresa? He struggled a little harder and blinked his eyes. In the grim darkness, he could see nothing.

She snapped the flashlight back on and he flinched, scrunching his eyes closed, wanting to turn his head away but unable to make the effort.

"He moved," the voice in the background said.

"Yes," she agreed.

"He's waking up, then. He'll be all right." The voice spoke some more, but it was lower and Bowman couldn't make out the words. The tones were comforting, though, like listening to an old friend tell a story you've heard many times before, the words disappearing inside the familiarity of the sounds.

"I'll be back," the voice said. Then the second flashlight clicked on in the background and the voice walked away with a few quiet parting words. After a moment, a door slammed with an air-sealed *whump,* a motor turned over in the darkness and wheels pulled away, crunching softly on dirt and rock.

"Bowman." Theresa again. The flashlight, off to the side this time, did not hurt so bad. It was a soft orange glow beyond his closed eyelids.

"Bowman." He blinked, and he could see her silhouette. But there was something wrong. Where was her hair? "God-damnit, Nate, wake up."

She set the flashlight down in the dirt, pointing away from them. He could see in the pale light that she had her hair pulled back tight against her head, secured in the back.

"Terry?" he said, his voice a raspy whisper.

"Yes, Nate, I'm here. Are you going to make it?"

"Yeah. Yeah, Terry, I guess so."

"Too bad," she said, and she sighed. "Damnit, Bowman, why did you have to do this?"

Do this. Do what? What was she talking about?

"I didn't—"

"Shut up," she said. The words came out dark and cold, like an ugly blemish long hidden and suddenly shoved into the light. Her voice sounded like something from a swamp.

"You did everything. Just shut up and save your strength. You're going to need it . . . for a little while." The flashlight clicked off and she walked away.

When he regained consciousness for the second time, he felt the rumble of thunder and sensed the afterimage of the lightning strike. The thunder faded slowly, and he realized he must be near a natural sound break that had sent an echo rolling back.

He felt better now, his head clearer, and when he blinked and opened his eyes, he could see the velvety, gray-orange glow of the city lights reflecting off a low bank of clouds.

Another bolt of lightning flashed. Bowman struggled, lifted his head slowly. After a few moments, he heard the thunder again, and the faint echo. He tried to sit up, but there was something wrong with his arms. He realized then that his hands were bound behind him. A hot pain throbbed in his wrists, shooting up his arms, shoulders, and neck to his head, where it pulsed from one temple straight through to the other.

He rested for a moment and breathed gently. Then he rolled onto his side and swung up into a sitting position. He felt pebbles and dirt fall from his back and he realized that he wasn't wearing a shirt.

He looked down. His feet and legs were bare, too. All he had on was a ragged pair of white boxers.

"Don't try to move. Your hands are tied. If you try to stand up, I'll hurt you."

She had returned, and she stood in front of him.

"There are two men with me," she said. "I believe you've met them before."

"The Mexican cop?"

"Señor Machado, yes. He is just down the road, waiting for the other, who will be arriving with an associate at any moment. So don't screw around, Nate."

"Other?"

"The blond man. His name is Schmirnoff, believe it or not. Andre Schmirnoff. You met him downtown. He and his brother followed you into the tunnels."

"I didn't know what happened to them, didn't want to find out," Bowman said.

"They split up. Andre went up one tunnel, his brother the other. His brother followed you, and drowned. Andre is very angry.

"He used to hunt, and he claims to have won an Olympic Medal in marksmanship. I believe it was a Bronze, though he has never said. He grew bored hunting half-tame animals and shooting paper targets. Now he plays a more dangerous game. He will want to kill you when he returns."

"Where are my clothes?"

"Pulled off when they fished you out of the wash."

He nodded. That made sense. It was all becoming clear. With sudden realization, he saw that she had been there in the background guiding things all along. Who else could it have been? Eisor? Perhaps, but Eisor was dead.

Bowman felt revulsion, nausea, a great screaming of emotion at her betrayal. He leaned back and breathed deeply. Terry? How could it have been Terry? But it was, and through the horrified tumult within, he knew he had to know why.

"What happened?" he asked.

"What happened? Haven't you read the history books? The white man came and took the land we settled."

"Jesus. What about us—you and me?"

"There is no us. There never was. Not really. There may have been a time, Nate, when I felt something for you. But that died long ago."

"What happened in Mexico?"

"At the *tinajas*?"

"Yes."

"You idiots stumbled onto something you shouldn't have. You were traveling in a land where you weren't welcome. Just like you and your people have always been trespassing here."

"John?"

"John was a nice guy. But stupid. Why was he taking pictures? You know, it's funny, Nate. I knew you two were going to be out there somewhere along the *Camino del Diablo*. And I thought about changing the arrangements I had made. Just in case. You've always been pretty harmless, and a good source of information. But why should I change my plans? Would you change yours for me?"

"Terry, I—"

"Shut up! Just shut up! My name is Theresa. Not Terry, Theresa. It's the name my mother gave me. And it was the name of her mother's grandmother, and the name of women in my family for hundreds of years before that. And you want to corrupt it. Just like you and your kind corrupt everything else."

"Corrupt? I'm not the one smuggling drugs across the line."

"You are such a fool, Nate. I wouldn't smuggle drugs, it's too risky."

"What then?"

"You want to know? Okay, Nate, I'll tell you. And then you will see how stupid you've been. You and your people. And how patient my people can be. We measure the time we wait not in minutes or hours like you do, or even in days. We measure it in generations.

"Do you know, at least, who my grandmother was? I know you saw Fountain, and after that, you went to see Burton. He would know. Did he tell you?"

Bowman remembered what the archaeologist had said to him. Now he understood, but he did not reply, wanting to hear it from her.

"My name is Theresa María Saldivar. My great-great-grandmother was Livia Montiel Salazar. Her grandfather was Jose Marìa Montiel. He was one of the true pioneers of Tucson. He owned all the land for fifteen miles to either side and below us, toward the city, and north up into the mountain. In his time he was a great rancher, with a large family and many strong sons.

"He was present at the signing of the Gadsden Purchase. He didn't realize then that he was witnessing the signing away of his future, and the future of his family.

"Within a few years, his land had begun to shrink. He lost all of his sons except one. Most of them were killed in fights with encroachers. It was always our family that was punished for those fights, usually by the death of a family member. And when we won a fight and killed one or two of them, then the whites retaliated for that.

"Jose died and his son gave up and moved to town. My mother was born in the house he built on the south side, and she lived there all her life. I was the first of my family to go to college.

"I decided to go to law school, and I became an attorney. That's when I learned how things really work.

"I didn't know at first. I wanted to do right, to defend the public. But slowly I realized that the public was not worth defending. So I quit and went back to school. You remember I went to Mexico City to study for a year?"

Bowman nodded.

"While I was there, I learned something that changed my life. It taught me that what I needed to defend, what I should have been defending all along, was my past.

"All my life I grew up with my mother whispering in my ear: 'You see all that, mi'jah, all that land?' And she would wave her hand toward the mountains. 'All that was ours. And it still is, mi'jah. Es suyo y mio.'

"Do you know how maddening it can be to a little girl standing behind the chain-link fence of a schoolyard? A schoolyard that is not even fun to play in because the ground is so hard and dry that grass will not grow on it, only the sticky weed we call goat's head, and if you fall, those little thorns will cling to your dress, ratty and frayed already, leaving a wide patch of stickers where you landed on the ground. And when you get home, your mother looks at you and scowls and says, 'What have you done?'

" 'All that, mi'jah, all that is yours.' Do you understand what that is like? No! You can't. And when you tell the class, tell them about your land, they laugh, laugh at the little girl in the dirty dress who thinks the city is hers.

"Now they will not laugh. They will not laugh, because very shortly this *will* be mine.

"In Mexico City, when I was not studying law at *el colegio,* I searched the archives. It is all there, Bowman, the whole history of this place. But of course it would mean nothing to you, because you could not read it.

"You haven't even learned the language of your own neighbor! You think yourselves superior, because you *choose* to remain as ignorant as a first-grader.

"In the archives I found what my mother told me would be there: the land grant to this property, with the stipulation that all *ejido* lands would start at the river and lie to the south. Do you understand, Bowman? All of that land, from the river to here, is mine."

He knew where he was now: Puma Canyon, nestled against the base of the Catalinas and climbing high and sheer into those craggy slopes.

"It is the land of my family. It is my birthright."

"But that's all history now," he said. "What are you going to do, tell the people in their homes down there that they have to leave because they're trespassing? How are you going to make them leave, Terry?"

"Don't call me that! Goddamn you, don't call me that." She backed away a few steps as she spat the words at him, and when she moved into the circle of light, he saw the chunk of black steel in her hand.

Her thumb twitched restlessly and cocked the trigger on the revolver.

"Theresa!" he said quickly. "Okay, Theresa? But how are you going to persuade them to move?"

"I won't," she said and flipped her ponytail in a regal way. "They can keep it. But this canyon—Puma Canyon—is mine.

"Do you see now? The canyon is undeveloped, and there are no families to remove. The land has been in the hands of the BLM, and now it sits for sale in a city-controlled trust. Ordinarily it would go to the highest bidder. A consortium headed by Porter Eisor along with Dino Diamante and a few others was going to be that bidder. The price really didn't matter much to them. They had arranged for financing and were prepared to top any other bid. But as you know, their leader was beheaded."

"Where do you fit in, Theresa?"

"I come in and sweep up the pieces. The consortium is shattered—without leadership—and a big chunk of their financing is gone. The whole project is in jeopardy.

"Some interesting articles are going to run in the papers over the next couple of days. A small but well-financed group is going to put in the highest bid. But that's not the story. The story is about a young *chicana* who has done good by the community and is reclaiming her birthright. I have, you see, copies of the land grant. I am one of the victims of racism and now I am rising from the ashes of the white man's assault. All I want is the land that is rightfully mine. And I'm even willing to pay for it. Cash."

"And Mexico?"

"That's where the cash comes from."

"What was it, Theresa? We saw the bag break open, the white stuff spill out in the night. What was it?"

"Does it really matter, Nate? It was something that can be resold at a profit. That's what counts. That and the fact that I'm going to get my land back."

"So John and I were just unlucky. We stumbled into the wrong place at the wrong time."

"*Mal suerte*. And I couldn't let you just stumble out. Call it manifest destiny, Nate. The deal had to be made."

Bowman shook his head but said nothing.

"The people who tried to catch you at the border work for me, they are my friends, they are my people. But they got word too late, and you slipped by."

"And Allen?"

"Señor Machado watched you make the phone call from the other side. By then, we were in constant communication. So right after you hung up, I called Allen, figuring he was the first one you would get in touch with. Knowing you wouldn't try to call me, I told him I was worried about you. Asked if he had heard from you.

"He said he'd just talked to you, but he didn't want to tell me any more about it. He said he had a bunch of phone calls to make. He was cagey. He sounded as if he was on to something. I didn't know how much he knew. He had to be eliminated."

"Eliminated." The word tasted foul in his mouth.

"They questioned him for quite some time, Bowman. They left no marks, but he went through considerable pain while you were driving home, and then stopping at the Council meeting. I was surprised to see you there. I thought I stalled you long enough."

"More bad luck," he said. "Who sabotaged the meeting?"

"People who work for me occasionally. It was expensive, but it was a minor price to pay to have the vote put off. If they had approved the sale of Puma Canyon to Eisor's consortium that night, I never would have had a chance. I sud-

172

denly found myself cash rich but without time to get the stories I needed into the newspapers. Those stories will start tomorrow afternoon or the next morning."

"Why did you send me to Eisor?"

"He happened to be standing in my office when you called. He heard my secretary announce the call over the intercom, and he ordered me to set up a meeting with you. It was then I decided the time had come to get rid of the fat man. God, I hated him. The price I had to pay. Every time he crossed behind me at a meeting or in the office, he would rub that huge stomach against my back. All I could think of was sinking a knife deep into his soft belly.

"But business comes first. And it took time to arrange. So I had it done right after you left. It was then that I sent them after you, but they missed. In any case, it worked out well. It cast more suspicion on you, relieved some of the pressure on me."

"Glad I could help."

"You're an asshole, Nate."

He nodded. "Why didn't you just have me killed earlier, along with Allen?"

She stared at him long and hard. "I probably should have."

"So what now?"

"Now I'm waiting for one more delivery. You'll wait with me. Then I'm going back to Mexico for a few hours. You're staying here."

Bowman nodded slowly, understanding.

"Do you see the walls?" she asked, grabbing the flashlight and swinging it over the scrubby desert around them. The area they were in was surrounded by the nearly invisible remains of melted adobe walls.

"These are all that remain of the original homestead on my family's ranch. And these mud lumps will be the foundation of a great resort. Three hotels and a golf course. Just as planned.

"And do you see that jeep trail?" She pointed the light out into the desert night. "That leads up to a small piece of land that will remain private. I will build my home there, with a superb view of both the canyon and the resort."

"Lovely," Bowman said. She looked at him coldly.

"And next to my home will be a small, fenced-in plot of desert that can never be developed. That condition will be in all the contracts. That patch of land must never be touched, because it is the graveyard of my ancestors, and the bones of my relatives rest there." She smiled grimly. "That is what I will say, anyway."

"Congratulations," Bowman said. She scowled at him again.

She opened her mouth as if to say more, but just then two sets of headlights flashed from out in the desert.

"I have some questions for you," she said. "Think about whether you want to answer them right away, or with the help of Señor Machado."

Then she turned and walked toward the vehicles that were working their way up the dirt road toward them. One was a car. The configuration of lights on the other was familiar to Bowman: two piercing beams, high up, and the row of KC's along the roof.

Lightning struck in the distance to the south. The bolt left a green glow imprinted on Bowman's vision, fading quickly. Thunder followed, closer now.

A storm was building in the warm summer night—

unusual at this late hour—and winds were kicking up dust and detritus from the desert floor.

The thick bank of clouds roiled overhead, suffused with that eerie glow. The clouds were bunching against the mountains, pressure building, the storm about to explode.

Bowman looked down at his almost naked body. She had walked away fully confident that he wouldn't try to run. The idea of escaping over the desert barefoot, without clothing, and with his hands bound, was unthinkable.

He looked off at the dirt road. The headlights were just pulling through the last turn, creating shifting shadows among the ocotillo, tumbleweed, and saguaro. She walked out to meet them. She glanced back in his direction, but he was in shadow, and he was sure she couldn't see him.

Bowman had been blessed with long arms, and at the moment, he was thankful for it. He lay down and slipped his hands to his hips. He arched his back, balancing on his shoulders, and forced his wrists down over his hips and past his thighs. Then he lay flat on his back, with his legs kicked up in the air—an absurd parody of the fetal position—and slipped his hands over his feet and ankles.

He looked across the desert. The headlights flicked off, and Bowman rose, head pounding and heart racing, and stepped past the mud-wall line, moving carefully through the desert into the night.

He had put about two hundred yards of hard desert behind him when he heard the angry shouts. He looked back and saw flashlights swinging across the ground where he had been. They were moving quickly from the car to the ruin, sweeping the desert around them with the beams.

A bolt of lightning cracked down, striking the desert

floor, thunder right on top of it. The wind came in great damp blasts that whipped his long hair around his head. Bowman looked up at the dark face of the mountain. Another bolt of lightning struck, then thunder again. In a moment a tiny orange light radiated from where the bolt had hit.

Bowman looked carefully in the direction of the black mountain for the first time. He saw other pockets of orange there, shimmering gently in the night, and the barely visible lines of smoke rising upward. He looked back.

There was a soft pattering in the distance. It grew louder as the wall of rain moved across the desert. Then the rain was upon him.

Bowman turned away from the valley, away from the city lights, toward the mountain. And he ran, ran up the canyon toward Babat Duag in the darkness.

Thirty

Bowman crashed through the pines. They were back there somewhere, and when he stopped, he could hear, beyond the rush of blood pounding in his ears, the sounds of the two pursuers; the Mexican cop and the other one, the hunter.

The rain had stopped as quickly as it started, leaving only the fires from lightning strikes to mark the storm on the dry mountainside.

In the distance below, the lights of Tucson glittered maddeningly. If he could cut left or right and climb up over the high, steep canyon walls, he might be able to work his way back down to the desert, then to the city. And safety.

But Puma Canyon's topography was, Bowman realized now, a horrible trap.

The walls of the canyon rose sheer on both sides, hundreds of feet high at places. Short of scaling them, the only way out was to follow the draw all the way to the mountaintop. There, a bank of radio towers blinked mutely in the night, the red lights a warning beacon for aircraft.

Climbing the rocks in darkness would be impossible.

Even if he were willing to try, he would be vulnerable and exposed. The pursuers would hear him climbing and find him with their flashlights. Then they would shoot him down quickly and efficiently, maybe burying his body in the soft sand of the wash, or, he thought, more likely planting him in Terry's "family graveyard."

As if in response to his thoughts, one of the flashlight beams swung a careful arc over the east wall of the canyon.

Bowman could see that they were moving quickly up the draw behind him. He couldn't wait in the darkness. There was no way to go but ahead.

He stumbled on up the canyon, moving in a way that was alien to him—softly, quietly, keeping low.

As he moved, he worked at the cord around his wrists. Soon it was loose, and he dropped it in the darkness. Brush and cactus scraped his near-naked body.

Ethnographers claimed that the mountain was called Babat Duag because it looked like a frog, rising in a dark hump from the desert. Bowman was clawing his way up the frog's back, and when he looked down again, the beams of the flashlights were closer.

Beyond the hunters, the splotches of fire grew, feeding off dry desert grass, forming a gapped wall of orange at the base of the mountain. Pockets of flame glowed above the ridge on either side of him.

Bowman knew that his only hope was to outdistance them, to make it to the mountain peak first.

If he were lucky, he might find someone there at the radio towers—a repairman, a camper, or if the fires were spreading, an emergency vehicle. If not, he would just have to try to lose his pursuers on the other side.

Two dirt trails led away from the tower. One wound

down the far side of the mountain; the other crossed the ridge to the east, weaving across the frog's back and down its bumpy head to Redington Pass.

If he couldn't find help at the radio towers, Bowman figured he would leave the hunters to choose between the two trails.

Maybe he could convince them to choose the wrong one.

Thirty-One

Bowman's eyes snapped open. His heart drummed. A noise echoed in his consciousness. Something in the distance, cutting through sleep. Then he heard it again. A scuffling on the trail behind him.

At the radio towers there had been nothing. He'd watched the mountainside in flames below.

Bowman had done his best to throw the hunters off, walking a few hundred feet up the trail toward Redington Pass, then backtracking in his own footsteps, staying to the rocks as he descended the backside of the mountain. But he knew it wouldn't throw them for long. If at all. And his feet were so torn and ragged that he had to stay on the trail now.

The hand was even worse. Running up the other side he had tripped, fallen, punctured the thick, fleshy pad at the heel of his palm. He'd had nothing to bandage it with. And the dirt. He had rubbed thick, brown soil all over himself—camouflage against the probing flashlights. The cut was gritty and uncomfortable, and part of the time he'd had to run with his hands clasped in front of him, pinching the wound closed. Finally the bleeding had eased. He'd been tired, and many times he'd felt like quitting. *Just keep going, man, just keep going*—the forest a darkened blur around him, his footsteps matching the heated rhythm of his breath.

At last he sat down alongside the trail, closing his eyes for just a moment to rest. How long had he slept? He didn't know.

The night sky was paling to the east, stars fading. A fine, rose-colored meridian severed the horizon.

Bowman looked west across the mountainside. A wide slope of barren, scrabbled rock stretched a couple of hundred yards in front of him. The field of shale sloped at a sharp angle. Apparently it was impassable. There was nowhere to gain safe footing on the shifting rock, and no vegetation to grab onto—nothing but a couple of barrel cactuses, squatting like short, meaty watchdogs at the bottom of the slope.

Beyond the cactuses, the slope ended abruptly. The black rock cliff dropped hundreds of feet below.

The trail paused here, then continued in a series of switchbacks up the mountain, around the slope, and back down into the trees on the far side.

Bowman held still, listening intently. The path receded behind him into the darkness of the pines. Then he heard it again. The hunters on the trail, no more than a few hundred yards behind him now. He started up the path, moving toward the switchbacks.

His feet stopped him. They were broken in many places, he was sure of that now. Several times he had felt a snap as he stumbled into rocks along the rough trail, breaking already broken toes.

The soles of his feet were scratched, scraped, and cut,

and with each step their shrieks of pain nearly shouted down the bellowing of his broken toes.

The switchbacks towered above him. Suddenly it seemed a huge distance to climb. Impossible.

Bowman looked over the bank of shale in front of him. If he could somehow scramble across the slope . . .

The way would be more painful than on the trail, but he'd gain time. They would have to go up and around. Or else make the risky climb after him.

In any case, if he took to the switchbacks, they would be on top of him almost at once. He wouldn't stand a chance.

Bowman looked back down the trail. He saw a shimmering movement in the darkness. He turned, climbed the embankment, and started across the rocky slope.

He was about a third of the way over when he heard the noise in the clearing behind him. He did not look back. He kept his eyes on the treacherous scarp beneath him, leaning in, clawing with both hands as he crabbed across.

He heard footsteps on the slope behind him. Following. He still did not look back, but concentrated on the western edge of the slope, the small clearing, and the stand of pines beyond.

The footsteps paused when a few feet onto the slope, then moved forward. He heard a great panting of breath, and the muttered, *"chinga, chinga"* with each exhalation. So Señor Machado was behind him.

For a moment he had a vision of the fat man scrambling across the slope in an ungainly, elephantine dance, and he almost looked back to confirm the image, but he resisted the urge, redoubling his concentration, trying to move faster. Machado was gaining on him.

Bowman was two-thirds of the way across when the footsteps behind him burst forward in a noisy scramble. Then the hand was at his shoulder.

He was knocked to his knees in the shale, the hand pressing down on him. He began to slide down the hillside. The cop clung to him, his grip digging into Bowman's shoulder.

"Señor," the cop panted, "you are mine."

Bowman twisted away. The cop yanked him back down by the neck, slamming him into the shale.

Then men both were sliding. Bowman felt the rocks scraping fiercely at his back. He drove the heel of his good hand into the ground and fought against the rocks with his bare feet.

The cop was on his stomach, kicking against gravity and clawing at the ground with his free hand.

If he'd only let go, Bowman thought, *we both might stop the slide.* But Machado seemed determined to hang on to him.

Bowman lifted his head, looking between his outstretched legs. They were slipping faster now, and the cliff's edge was just a few feet away.

Then Bowman realized it was too late. The rocks were sliding under him, and he had gained too much momentum. Even if the cop let go now, he would not be able to stop in time.

The cop looked down for the first time and reached the same conclusion.

He let go of Bowman, drawing his hand back as if snakebit, and scrambled madly against the sliding rocks.

Then they were at the edge. The cop, a little below him, looked back at Bowman with a sad, hurt look. Bowman twisted onto his belly, lunging against the short strip of hard rock at the base of the slope, diving with arms out-

stretched, eyes wincing, face drawing away from the antic-
ipated impact.

He heard the high-pitched shriek, fading quickly as the
cop disappeared over the precipice.

The sound of a distant pop followed.

Then nothing.

Bowman clung to a barrel cactus, the thorns piercing his
forearms and hands, the weight of his body driving the
thick hooks deep inside.

He lay on his bare stomach, scratched and bleeding, pain
shrieking through his forearms and across the long trunk of
his body.

He looked back the way he had come, half-expecting to
see the blond man standing at the side of the slope, smiling,
the gun raised and centered, waiting only for the look of
recognition in Bowman's eyes. But the trail was empty.

Then, through the trees, he heard the unmistakable noise
of footsteps on the rocky trail. The sun had risen higher
now, and he could see, farther up, the pale image of the
hunter on the trail.

Bowman realized that the blond man must have taken
the eastern fork at the radio tower, then doubled back and
followed the Mexican cop when he realized Bowman had
gone the other way. He must have heard the cop's scream,
since he was moving quickly down the path.

Suddenly Bowman felt terribly tired—a deep fatigue
that went beyond physical exhaustion and clear to his
spirit, to his instinct for self-preservation. What was the
point? he wondered wearily. If Terry could do this, what
kind of a world was it, and why stay around? For a moment
he considered letting go of the barrel cactus. He could simply spin away and slip off the cliff's edge, taking one last

look at the magnificent desert wilderness in the graying dawn light.

He rejected the idea. If the bastard was going to kill him, fine. But meanwhile, he was going to scramble over to the other side of the slope and head down the trail. That's what he told himself, anyway, as he peeled his arms from the cactus, turned his back on the hunter, felt for solid footing, and began working his way up and across the shale.

Then he heard the thin *snap* as a gun was half-cocked, and *snap*—fully cocked.

Bowman paused. He felt a strong urge to turn and look back, but willed himself to ignore it. Instead, he looked ahead. Only a few more feet. He concentrated on the slope's edge and began moving again.

He reached up and grabbed hold of a rock, pulling himself off the slope and toward the clearing. The rock gave way with a loud crack and rolled past him as he slipped back down. He looked up and saw the kick of dust where his head would have been, the sound of the gunshot echoing.

Then Bowman was grabbing at another rock, scrambling into the clearing and bolting toward the cover of the trees, the thin sound of the gun being recocked fading behind him.

Thirty-Two

The dome rose from the desert like a gigantic glass-and-steel terrapin, its shell twinkling in the sunlight.

The first biosphere experiment had been a tremendous success. Financially. Despite plenty of criticism from the press, crowds of tourists had flocked to the huge terrarium, gawking at the eight human guinea pigs who had locked themselves inside.

But after the first crew emerged, the novelty wore off and the crowds quit coming. The second and third biosphere experiments had been cut short, and number four never got off the ground.

Now the abandoned structure sat quietly in the Arizona desert. A security guard drove north from Tucson on the weekends to run off hormonally charged teenagers looking for a place to have sex and vandalize. A tall, chain-link fence had been erected around the area.

It was Monday, and Bowman realized that the chance of a security guard being around was slim. But if he were lucky, he might find a live telephone somewhere inside the sprawling complex.

Ten feet of chain link stood between him and a possible haven. And he knew he could not climb it.

It was all Bowman could do to walk now, and the idea of hooking his shattered toes into the thin links of galvanized wire was unthinkable.

He looked back over his shoulder. There was a rustling in the sage along the road behind him. Then the blond man stepped out of the brush a hundred yards back. He was smiling as he raised the pistol.

Bowman cut to the left, running toward the palo verdes by the fence. He felt a gentle tug at his hair, heard the sound of the shot. Then he was among the trees, crashing through the clutching branches, racing past the fence.

The palo verdes thinned quickly; apparently they had been planted near the road to discourage people from exploring the fence line.

Bowman shambled over the dirt and rock, through the sage, trying to keep his weight off his broken toes. He heard a rustling behind him. The hunter was pushing through the branches of the palo verdes, going slowly, cautiously, from the sound of it. Bowman followed the fence.

The hole was about three feet in diameter, starting at the the dirt and forming a sharp-edged, oblong gash in the chain link. Bowman had seen plenty of holes just like it in the fence along the border. But this one had probably been cut by a different kind of mule—the teenage American ass.

He wiggled through the hole and ran down the gently sloping hill toward the biosphere.

Up close, Bowman could see that the complex was in bad shape. Many of the glass panels were broken, lying shattered on the floor inside. The sidewalk circling the structure was strewn with debris: empty beer cans, glass shards, lengths of steel framework.

Bowman looked back over his shoulder. The hunter was just emerging from the trees, cautiously entering the clearing. Bowman looked up and down the walkway. Then, carefully avoiding the broken glass, he ducked into the biosphere.

It was dark inside, darker than Bowman expected. He looked up at the remaining panes of glass. They were caked with a hard, dark substance. Sunlight filtered through dimly.

The complex comprised a number of sections. In its heyday, there had been an ocean setting and a rain forest, as well as a desert and a savanna. Each had existed separately, linked by chambers for the "researchers" to pass through.

Bowman was standing in the ocean complex now. It was a mess. Trash everywhere. The water had been drained long ago, and he was standing at the bottom of what appeared to be an enormous swimming pool. The floor and sides of the pool were coated with the same black substance that covered the glass panels. Mold, he realized—mold that had dried and turned hard.

There was a ladder at the far end of the empty ocean. Bowman picked his way around the debris and climbed it. He stood among the fake rocks that formed a grotto at one end of the ocean. It reminded him of an elaborate zoo habitat. Or maybe a movie set. But these rocks were covered with graffiti. "Bios-fear!" someone had written. And, "Party Dome." There was also the usual assortment of scatological words and phrases.

Deep in the recess of the fake cave there was a door, and

again Bowman was reminded of a zoo cage, complete with feeding door. The door was ajar and the hallway beyond it dark. Bowman looked back the way he had come. He could see the shadow of the hunter, moving cautiously along the side of the sphere toward the hole where he had entered. Bowman stepped through the doorway.

At the far end of the hall stood another metal ladder. Bowman looked back again. The door to the cave was a shimmering rectangle in the distance now. He thought he heard faintly the sound of glass crunching against the ocean floor.

Bowman ascended the ladder. It ran up a vertical tunnel, and he climbed quickly into the darkness.

His head banged into the steel door with a *thunk*. The door was a round portal with a big metal wheel for a lock. He felt for the wheel, grabbed it and twisted. It turned slowly. Then stopped. He threw himself against it, twisting with all he had. Nothing. Stuck. He pushed against the door. Still locked.

Bowman scrambled back down the ladder. He felt panic scratching at his insides, reaching up to clutch his throat. He fumbled around in the darkness on the ground, trying to find a steel bar or a piece of pipe—something to use as a lever. He looked toward the doorway. In the dim light under the dome, the blond man worked his way slowly across the empty ocean. Then he knelt and rubbed one hand along the ground. In the other hand he held a gun.

Bowman continued to search the floor. There had to be something. His fingers bumped hard against a tubular piece of metal. A pipe. He gripped it firmly and pulled. It didn't budge.

He felt along the length of the pipe, and after a few feet,

it curved at a joint and entered the wall. He yanked at the base, twisting hard against the joint.

Then he heard a scraping noise, and when he looked up, the hunter's blond hair was just appearing at the top of the ladder. Gun first, the hunter climbed out of the empty ocean.

Bowman was trapped. The hunter was walking slowly toward the recess of the cave, blocking the only exit.

Bowman pulled on the bar one more time, willing it to snap from the wall, driving against it with his heels, pain shrieking from feet to shoulders. Nothing. The pipe did not even tremble.

The hunter ducked into the cave, moving forward carefully, allowing his eyes to adjust to the light.

Watching the man step toward the door, Bowman had an idea. He didn't know that it would work, but it was his only chance.

He tried to remember what the door looked like. Did it open in or out? He ran down the hallway, his footsteps slapping echoes into the darkness.

The hunter jerked his head up, stepped to the side, and raised his gun in the direction of the sound. Then he disappeared, crouching into the darkness of the cave.

The door opened in, and Bowman hit it on the run, driving his shoulder against steel. It creaked resistantly, then swung forward. He felt a slap, then a thrumming, and heard the gunshot, and another. Then the door was closed and Bowman was fumbling with the latch, twisting it, hoping that it locked from the inside, and that on the outside there was just a handle and a keyhole. A rapid burst of gunfire knocked on the steel door and Bowman threw himself to the side.

It was as dark as an abandoned mine shaft in the room. The bullets had not penetrated the door. He heard a scrabbling noise at the handle. Then curses and more gunshots, apparently aimed at the latch, which held. Then nothing.

Thirty-Three

Bowman stood atop the dome, the morning sun already beating down hard, sweat breaking out on his forehead and in his armpits. The glass and steel at his feet were warming quickly.

He had groped around in the darkness of the corridor and finally found a loose piece of steel framing. Using it for a lever he had forced the lock open and crawled through the open hatch. He'd found another steel ladder, and another, and eventually had pushed through a glass hatch to the roof of the huge dome. But the hunter had seen him, and followed, and now he was climbing rapidly up the ladder below.

A hot breeze pulled Bowman's hair back from his forehead. He looked down on the desert. It was, above all else, a beautiful view. To the southwest, *Cañon del Oro* dipped in craggy slopes. Beyond was the north face of the Catalinas.

Bowman looked back toward the ladder. He could see dimly through the dark glass panels that the hunter was climbing inexorably toward him.

He looked around the roof of the dome. Nothing. No

debris. There was only slick, hot glass and steel to stand on, and sheer edges at each side. *Nowhere to run to, baby, nowhere to hide.*

He stepped away from the hatch and walked toward the western edge of the dome.

What the hell, at least I'll die looking west. He glanced at his battered feet. *And with my boots off.*

Bowman grinned, looking out over the sand and sage, caliche and cactus, toward the Tortolita Mountains. It was indeed a spectacular vista.

As he stepped forward, the panel gave underfoot. The glass slipped down in its rusted frame, nearly popping out into the oblivion below. Bowman shifted his weight in mid-stride, and hopped beyond it to the next girder.

He looked back toward the hatch. Through the dirty glass he could see the hunter, nearly to the top. Suddenly it was clear to him. There might be a way out.

As the blond man popped his head out of the hatch, Bowman lay very still.

He was on his stomach, his face turned away from the man, and it was all he could do to resist the urge to turn and look. He heard a grunt as the man climbed out of the dome, and the soft, careful footsteps as he moved forward.

Bowman could imagine the gun, out in front, aimed precisely at the back of his head. He kept still, and now he held his breath, willing himself to lay motionless.

"Mister Bowman." The voice was very close. "Why do you lie there? Is this a silly game you are playing?"

Bowman stared out at the valley, listening hard, counting footsteps.

"You have disappointed me. You did so very well until these last few minutes. Then you walked into your own trap. Ah well, there will be other animals, *better* animals—" then there was a shriek of tearing metal, a snap of glass breaking, and the startled yelp as he fell.

Bowman rose and spun around. He saw the fingers, clawing at the lip of the empty frame. He moved forward cautiously. The hunter hung there, staring stupidly at the emptiness below. He looked up at Bowman.

"A hand?" he asked, his voice strained.

Bowman lay very flat for leverage. Then paused. The hunter had dropped his gun and probably wasn't as dangerous now. But this man had killed Allen, and Eisor. And how many others? Bowman knew he could simply walk away. But then the hunter might pull himself up and out and come after him again. Or he could stomp the fingers and watch him fall. That would probably be best. Though he wasn't sure he had the stomach for it.

"Please," the man said.

Bowman reached out a hand, and the hunter grabbed it.

He was a heavy man, and Bowman didn't have much strength left. He tried to pull the hunter up, but he started slipping. The hunter let go of the edge with his other hand, and Bowman could see that the jagged glass was covered with blood. The hunter clung to his arm with both hands now.

Bowman was sweating, and as the hunter slipped slowly down his arm, his cut hands left thin tracks of blood.

Bowman swung his other arm over and grabbed the hunter's wrist. The man's eyes turned cold and his grip suddenly grew stronger.

"Can't make it," he gasped. "You killed my brother . . . Least you can do is join me."

Bowman felt himself sliding toward the edge, leverage slipping away. He looked down at the blond man, looked into his eyes. He didn't know this man—this man who was trying to kill him and whose life he was trying to save. If he held on, the hunter would pull him over the edge; if he let go, the man would fall to his death. He remembered that Terry had told him the hunter's name.

"Schmirnoff, right?" Bowman asked, through gritted teeth.

The blond man nodded.

"I myself," Bowman said, "prefer tequila." And he let go.

Thirty-Four

He was in bad shape and he knew it. He had pulled the shirt and pants off the dead hunter. The shoes were too small, but he eased the socks on over his painfully swollen feet. Then he had walked up the lonely dirt road, away from the abandoned complex, shambling along in the dirt like some tall, shaggy survivor of the Apocalypse—a battered and bruised Sasquatch, far from home.

When he reached the state highway, he stood on the shoulder of the road with his thumb out and waited for a ride.

Bowman counted thirty-seven vehicles, sixteen of them trucks with open beds—all with license plates from the United States—before the shiny, white Mercedes stopped. Its plates were from Sonora, Mexico.

The driver spoke perfect English, and he showed a great deal of concern for Bowman's condition. He asked repeatedly if Bowman wanted to go to a hospital.

"No," he answered. "Not yet, anyway."

Bowman knew the man was right. He needed a doctor. And a great deal of rest. He felt that he had been running below empty for days, burning away at the core of his power supply. He figured the events of the past few hours had cut weeks off his life. Bowman smiled. He was content just to be here.

He intended to go to a hospital, but there was someplace else he had to go first, someone he had to see.

The driver dropped him off at home, and Bowman thanked him. He knew better than to insult the man by offering money.

"*Gracias, amigo*," he said simply.

"*Vaya bien*," the man said and drove away.

Bowman washed slowly, easing into a warm tub and caressing his rough skin with soap. Every part of him hurt, each muscle ached, every inch of skin seemed to be cut or scratched, and the bath sponge felt like steel wool.

He dried off and sat on the edge of the tub, doctoring his wounds. He spread ointment over both feet, covered them with cotton pads, and wrapped them in bandages. He gooped up his cut hand and taped a thick cotton pad over it as well.

Then he called the artist.

"Durand," he said, "I need wheels. Can I borrow your truck?"

"Sure," the artist said. "Come on by."

Before Bowman could continue, the artist had clicked off. He pressed re-dial.

"Studio," the artist answered immediately.

"Durand, this is Nate."

There was a pause. Finally the artist spoke. "I thought you were coming over to borrow my truck," he said, with a touch of suspicion in his voice.

"I'd like to borrow it," Bowman said. "But I can't get over there. Can you swing by?"

Another pause.

"Sure. You at home?"

"Yes."

Another click, and the line went dead. A little while later, he was dropping the artist back at his studio and driving south across the city, toward the reservation.

Thirty-Five

"Coming. Coming!" the historian called. "Don't leave, I'll be right there!"

Bowman's stomach tightened in a sick knot. He waited, and in a moment the security port opened and Fountain's expectant face appeared.

The historian's look turned to a painful grimace when he saw Bowman.

"Nate," he said quietly. Then he closed the hatch. Bowman waited on the porch. A minute passed, then another. Finally the door swung open slowly.

"I could have run, you know," the historian said softly, and then he turned and led Bowman straight back to the study.

They sat opposite each other in the tall, overstuffed chairs, staring at the floor for what seemed like a long time—long enough that the historian began to shift uncomfortably.

"How did you know?" Fountain asked at last.

"I didn't at first. I guess I'd have found out. You were in the car, weren't you?"

Fountain nodded. He was not looking at Bowman. He stared at the area around Bowman's feet, refusing to meet his eyes.

"The problem was," Bowman said, "I got stuck thinking about the smuggling. I forgot the first rule: the story's never what you think it is. I should have known, should have realized. She told me, but I didn't believe her. I figured she was lying, like she'd done about so many other things. Suddenly I realized my mistake—at the biosphere, of all places."

Fountain glanced up, a look of interest in his eyes, then quickly returned his gaze to the floor.

"Pseudoscience, I know. But I got to thinking about the amount of technology involved, the incredibly expensive technology. That's when it occurred to me. They were smuggling something *into* Mexico. Nobody smuggles *drugs* into Mexico. So she'd been telling the truth, and it had to be something else.

"When I was here on the night of the storm, you got up and left the room. You were gone a long time, longer than it would take to get a couple of drinks. Long enough to make a phone call.

"And out at the ruin, she knew I'd seen you, and that I was going to see Burton afterward. You were the only one who knew that."

"Yes, Nate," the historian said. "You've followed the evidence precisely."

"What was it?" Bowman said. "We saw the bag spill open, saw the white stuff fall out. What was it?"

"Peanuts," Fountain said.

"Peanuts?"

"Peanuts," Fountain nodded. "Packing chips—little kernels of styrofoam to protect very sensitive equipment."

"So it was some kind of computer part, some little mechanical aberration used in those fucking missiles. And you were selling it to who? The Cubans? The Russians?"

"The buyers were North Korean, actually, with a Mexican friend of Theresa's acting as the middleman. Not that it matters. Don't you understand, Nathaniel, that all of this is just future history? It was a computerized guidance mechanism for a missile prototype I've been working on. If they didn't buy it here, they'd buy it somewhere else."

"So that's it," Bowman said. "You did it for money? Why? You have enough, you live comfortably."

"Money," the historian scoffed. "Money itself is meaningless, boring."

"Men commit atrocities for it."

"Don't you see that there is no morality involved in the acts of men?" Fountain asked heatedly. "We are capable only of destruction and cruelty and violence. Each of us is Ozymandias, crumbling slowly to the sand. The only measure of any man's life is the length of his legacy.

"It isn't the money. It's what I'm going to do with it. Enough cash to fund a new building for the Historical Society. A building in my name. A building that will outlive me by a hundred years or more. And enough money to get my books published by the big houses. Then those bastards at the university can sit and stew.

"Don't you see, Nate? I've never received the recognition I deserve. Not from the ivory tower. They won't touch my work. And when I'm gone, if I haven't done something about it, all my research, all my efforts, all my writing, will fade to obscurity. Why should my statue crumble faster than anyone else's? I don't deserve that!"

Bowman shook his head slowly. He was too tired to care about the historian's convulsions. He felt worn to his soul. Tired of men. Tired of mankind.

"It's not going to play out that way, Toppy."

The historian looked up, panicked.

"It can't," Bowman went on. "It's not just me. It's the photos. They're already at *The Weekly*—developed and blown up by now. No matter what happens, they'll see the people by the plane. It was you with Terry, right?"

The historian nodded glumly.

"I'm sorry," Bowman said. Then he was interrupted by the doorbell.

"You expecting someone?"

"Her." Fountain said. "She's delivering the last payment."

"I'll get it," Bowman said.

As he walked out of the room, the historian rose and crossed toward the fireplace, and John Ringo's pistol.

Bowman made his way through the maze of hallways to the front door. He was reaching for the door knob when he heard the noise. A loud report echoing from deep inside the house. He closed his eyes and leaned against the door, grinding his teeth.

It was probably better this way. Fountain wouldn't have made it in prison. And the historian was an accomplice, no matter how you looked at it. Better this way, maybe, but it sure as hell wasn't right.

Bowman opened the door.

She was more than startled to see him; she was stunned.

Her jaw dropped and her shoulders jerked back. Her eyes flicked around as if looking for a way out.

Bowman quickly grabbed her by the front of her shirt, pulling her forward, off balance, into the house. He ripped the bag from her shoulder and shoved her against the wall. He clawed the purse open and dumped its contents on the floor. Nothing. No gun.

"Where's Toppy?" she asked.

"Gone." Bowman said.

"May I turn around now?"

"Yes. But don't do it too quickly. And don't screw around. I'm stronger than you, and my hands aren't tied this time. And you don't have a gun."

"Gun? What for?"

"Sure," he said, moving to a phone on an end table near the doorway. "Whatever you say, Terry." He saw the look of fire in her eyes when he said it.

"I wasn't going to have them do anything to you, Nate," she said. "Nothing terrible. I'm not a horrible person."

He cocked an eyebrow at that.

"I just had a few questions. About the film, the photos Vyking took. Have they been developed? Do you know if they came out?" He saw the fear in her eyes.

Bowman paused with the phone in his hand, one finger on the button.

"The photos, Terry? The photos are at *The Weekly*. By now they've been developed and blown up. Mac knows some of the story, and no matter what happens, it's all over. You're finished. You were finished yesterday. You just didn't know it yet."

Her jaw clenched, lips trembling slightly. Her eyes were

filled with rage and panic and pain. The eyes of a coyote caught in a steel-jaw trap.

Then her expression shifted, turning cold. For the first time, Bowman saw her suddenly shifting temper—an aspect in her that had once attracted him—for what it really was: madness.

"Listen, Nate, if it's all over, let me go," she said quietly. "Can't you see my side? I never had the things I wanted. You . . . they always took them away. Why not just let me go and never come back? In Mexico I can disappear."

Bowman stared at her long and hard. She seemed all at once a sad and lonely creature.

But that wasn't enough.

"John is dead," he said. "And Allen. You did that. You are responsible."

"It wasn't my fault!" she screamed.

"I remember watching the National Guard shoot those students at Kent State." Bowman said. "I was a freshman, on my way to class, just passing by.

"That was the first time I saw anyone die. It pushed me down a long, narrow path, and eventually life didn't really have any meaning at all. I had to take meaning from escape, from going, from diving as deep as possible into the harsh wilderness, trying to find something worth living for in the angry beauty there. Life was just too much most of the time, the world had gotten to be too fucking crazy, and the only thing I could do was to leave it behind—to go where no one talks to you, and the dunes only whisper to the wind.

"John and I were just walking that road at the *tinajas*. Allen was doing his job. But it has meaning, it must. When someone kills your friends, you have to do something or

there isn't meaning to anything, not to the smogged streets
or the rain-washed sand, or the bed you sleep in."

He saw the look of scorn in her eyes.

"Too much of a speech for you? Fine."

And he dialed the three-digit number.

Thirty-Six

Bowman wrote most of the story sitting up in a hospital bed.

With his feet resting gently on two soft pillows, a laptop computer in front of him, the modem line running to a telephone jack, he banged away for hours at a time.

It took three days, and he wrote nearly a hundred pages. The editors would pare it down, cut the fat, check the facts, and confirm the most sensitive parts.

Mac talked to him on a second phone line almost hourly, trying angles, poking and prodding at the story and at Bowman's mind, always pushing him to think, clarify, and rethink.

His cut hand grew stiff and tired quickly. It was stitched with thirty-two loops of black thread, and he could feel it ache as the healing began. His feet weren't as bad as he'd thought at first. Three toes broken on the left, one on the right, and a jumble of minor cuts and abrasions. The injured toes on the left foot were each broken in a couple of places. They had been set, with small aluminum splints taped around them.

The fire on the mountain burned for a couple of days. Bowman watched the smoke through his hospital window, and at night he could see the unearthly orange glow. Finally a heavy rain came up from the gulf and squelched it.

The story eventually ran twelve pages, with a large photo filling the front page of *The Weekly:* an image of the smugglers in the night, with a boxed blowup showing Fountain and Theresa by the plane.

The part about the historian's involvement and suicide was difficult to write, but he worked through it.

Then there was round after round of questioning by investigators from the Justice Department, the state attorney general's office, local and county police.

Arrests had been made, and the attorney general was publicly promising grand-jury indictments.

The development at Puma Canyon was dead for now, and there was talk of turning it into a wildlife refuge. But the way Bowman figured it, it wouldn't take long for the Diamantes to turn that around. Someone would rise up to take Eisor's place, and the bulldozers would roll on.

When he left the hospital, Bowman took a few weeks off work, licking his wounds. He lay low in the swamp-cooled darkness of his old adobe bungalow.

The cops fished his Land Cruiser out of the muddy, nearly dry riverbed, and Bowman had it towed to his mechanic, Norm.

"Well," the mechanic said, scratching his balding head, then tugging at one handle of his thick blond mustache. "It'll run, but it ain't gonna be pretty."

"Kind of a tradition with me," Bowman said.

He read some books that he'd had lying around forever,

and reread Cormac McCarthy's *Blood Meridian,* the greatest novel of the American West.

In the afternoons he watched the unstoppable dark clouds building in the south, roiling up from the gulf on the monsoon winds, meeting the immovable object of the Catalinas and exploding in torrential rains. Sometimes he sat on his porch through the storm with wind and rain beating him cold and ragged.

Finally he went to the office. He did not notice the light switch or the metal desk just inside the door, and he carefully avoided looking down at the spot where Allen had lain.

He received grim congratulations and a few quiet looks of sympathy as he wandered through the place.

He walked back to his dugout and sat there for a while, staring at the pile of mail on his desk.

Then he went through Layup to Mal's office—Allen's old office.

He told the new editor what he planned to do. Mal nodded approval and asked if he needed anything.

"Desert," Bowman said, and walked out.

He headed north and east, fighting traffic across town. Near the end of Speedway, he turned left and crossed the Rillito, then took a right, heading toward the mine and the gap at Redington Pass.

A convenience store squatted in the dust at the roadside just before the blacktop turned to dirt. Bowman pulled in. He filled the tank and both jerry cans with gas. Inside, he paid, and bought five plastic jugs of drinking water. He pulled the Land Cruiser around to the air and water hoses, checked the tires, and filled the spare water can.

He climbed back into the Land Cruiser and switched on the ignition. The vehicle jumped to life and rumbled beneath him. Bowman sat with both hands on the wheel, not moving. Thinking about her.

How could he have missed it? How could he not have seen? Maybe he had seen, but had chosen to ignore it, chosen to lie to himself.

If she could stand to have the fat man pawing her, all the while hiding her revulsion, why should he have thought himself any different?

Just another blind fool, he thought. *Blind, ugly fool.*

He switched the ignition off, set the emergency brake, and walked back into the store.

"Forget something?" the little man in the white smock asked.

"Lottery ticket."

"Cash payoff, or annuity in fifty yearly payments?"

Bowman smiled. "Better make it payments. Don't want to be greedy."

The clerk took his dollar and gave him the slip of paper.

Bowman walked back out to the parking lot, and crossed to the Land Cruiser. The slip of paper between his fingers fluttered in the hot breeze.

Without looking at the lottery numbers, he slowly crumpled the ticket into a tight ball. As he climbed into the Land Cruiser, he threw the slip away.

Bowman started the vehicle and pulled onto the road. Soon the blacktop ended and he was crashing down the strip of dirt, a great rooster tail of dust billowing behind.

The dirt road wound up the canyon, past the mine, then down the far side of the pass and across the wide San Pedro Valley.

Beyond the San Pedro, he stopped the Land Cruiser, climbed out, and locked the hubs for four-wheel drive.

In the distance, down the jeep trail, the Galiuro Mountain Range sat stoically in the summer sun.

The Galiuros were a scrappy stretch of low mountains, all red rock and craggy cliff faces, with brush and cactus and not much else. Abbey had worked there once, in one of his various incarnations as a seasonal employee of the U.S. Forest Service—before he was able to earn a meager living from his writing.

The Galiuros were a protected-wilderness area, and the jeep trail ended at the base of the desolate range.

There, Bowman would park the Land Cruiser among the mesquite and the palo verde—just switch it off, really, and leave it where the trail ended.

Then he would get out and walk. And walk.